a *Poppy Creek* novel

RACHAEL BLOOME

Cover design: Ana Grigoriu-Voicu with Books-design

Editing: Beth Attwood

Proofing: Krista Dapkey with KD Proofreading

SERIES READING ORDER

The Clause in Christmas

The Truth in Tiramisu

The Secret in Sandcastles

The Meaning in Mistletoe

The Faith in Flowers

The Whisper in Wind

The Hope in Hot Chocolate

Shorty,

For continually inspiring me and others to make a difference in the world

LETTER FROM THE AUTHOR

Dear Friends,

This story came at an interesting time in my life. I hit so many roadblocks trying to publish this novel—both professionally and personally—there were times I wasn't sure I'd be able to finish, even though it was dear to my heart. It took prayer, perseverance, and a whole lot of hope. And in hindsight, I realized I was walking a journey similar in spirit to my characters, Vick and Lucy, which was both humbling and encouraging.

Going through trials or hardship isn't easy, but there's always hope. I'm reminded of Isaiah 40:31:

"But those who hope in the Lord will renew their strength. They will soar on wings like eagles; they will run and not grow weary, they will walk and not be faint."

For anyone struggling, know you're not alone. If you ever need a listening ear, I love hearing from my readers. You can reach me at hello@rachaelbloome.com

Until then,

Happy Reading!

Rachael Bloome

CHAPTER 1

Lucy Gardener sat in her shimmering gold convertible, gazing at the palatial inn that had occupied her full attention for the last several months.

Sunlight streamed through bronze and amber leaves, warming the ruddy bricks of the Georgian-style exterior and glinting off tall windows flanked by pristine white shutters.

For the first time in her life, Lucy felt a twinge of pride. Decorating the newly renovated inn from top to bottom, being careful to blend modern comfort with the building's historic heritage, hadn't been an easy task.

Especially since she had zero formal training.

Her eldest brother, Jack, who owned the Whispering Winds Inn, had plucked her from a job staging homes for their father's real estate business. She'd always had an eye for design, but never had any particular career aspirations, acquiescing to join the family business at her parents' urging.

According to her mother, the position was merely temporary, anyway—a stepping stone until she settled down with a good provider. Which couldn't happen too soon, if Elaine Gardener had her way.

Lucy shuddered at the thought of melding into her mother's role of consummate hostess and socialite, but she didn't have a better plan for her life.

Not that it mattered.

She reached inside her Prada bag and pulled out an ivory business card with a simple black font.

Ashton Neurological Clinic.

Her primary care physician had handed it to her earlier that morning with stoic professionalism, explaining why she needed to see the specialist in Los Angeles. It wasn't until he began listing the possible results of an MRI that his armor cracked, revealing misty eyes and a faint warble in his voice.

In all the years Dr. Dunlap had been the family physician, she'd never once seen the man get emotional.

That's what scared her the most.

Stuffing the card in the bottom of her purse, she climbed out of the driver's seat, her heeled boots crunching a pile of dry, crinkly leaves.

A crisp fall breeze rustled through the sycamore trees, lifting her spirits along with the fringed edges of her scarf.

Squaring her shoulders, she tilted her chin toward the cheerful sun brightening the clear blue sky and summoned a smile.

Lucy Gardener didn't worry about the future; she lived in the present, savoring everything life had to offer—for however long that may be.

She skipped up the wide steps of the inn, making her way toward the kitchen in the back, following the mouthwatering aroma of fresh coffee and buttery pancakes.

Kat Bennet stood at the state-of-the-art stove, attempting to flip a flapjack without a spatula. She gripped the griddle with a white-knuckled grasp and closed her eyes.

"Are you sure you want to do that?" Jack teased. "We all remember what happened to the last one." His gaze fell to the floor, where Fitz, a handsome husky mix, wagged his tail in anticipation of the next failed attempt.

"Hush," Kat scolded, widening her stance. "Third time's the charm."

"You mean *sixteenth,*" Jack corrected.

Kat eased open her eyelids just long enough to shoot him a playful scowl.

Lucy watched the exchange with amusement. As soon as she'd met the fiery redhead, she knew her brother had found a woman who could handle his special brand of humor—and dish it back in equal measure.

Although they weren't an obvious couple to the common observer—her brother's hulking, six-foot-four frame towered over Kat's petite five-six figure—they were a perfect match. And Lucy had never seen her brother more in love, or happier.

Lucy held her breath as Kat counted to three, flicked her wrists, and flung the flapjack high above her head.

It tumbled gracefully in the air before floating back to the center of the griddle.

Lucy cheered, and Kat's eyes flew open, sparkling at her success. "I did it!"

"Congratulations," Jack said sincerely, kissing her cheek. "But the real test is how it tastes."

"Thank goodness Lucy is here, since you can't be trusted as an impartial judge." Kat welcomed her into the conversation with a wide grin, motioning for her to take a seat at the expansive center island.

As Lucy settled on the barstool, Kat poured a cup of coffee and slid it across the marble countertop.

"Your brother is teaching me how to make his famous flapjacks. I plan to serve them to our first guest, who's arriving in three days. Three days! Can you believe it?" Kat's excitement spilled out of her like champagne bubbles fizzing over the edge of a glass.

Lucy smiled, finding her enthusiasm undeniably endearing.

Even though they'd decided to limit bookings to half capacity for the first month in order to ease into things, Lucy knew how long Kat had waited for this moment. She'd been dreaming about opening an inn for years, and the renovations had taken longer than expected.

Lucy couldn't even imagine Kat's level of emotion, so close to having her dream become a reality. If she were honest with herself, Lucy had never been that passionate about anything. Even her YouTube channel, *Life with Lucy,* was purely for kicks. It had started as a means to chronicle the renovation process, and over time, she posted anything and everything that struck her fancy.

But it was hardly a passion project. Not like the inn was for Kat, who'd thrown her entire heart and soul into every detail. She even planned to offer the most luxurious suite to a special guest for free, once a month, as her way of giving back. In fact, their first guest would be one such honoree.

That was just one of the many things Lucy admired about the generous, kindhearted woman, whom she hoped would become an official part of the family one day.

As the youngest sibling with five older brothers, Lucy had always wanted a sister. And Jack couldn't have chosen better. Now, if only he'd get his act together and propose already.

Not that she was one to give advice. In the romance department, she was as hopeless as her brothers. Although she'd been on plenty of dates in her twenty-five years, no one had grabbed her attention… until recently.

Unfortunately, he couldn't be any less interested.

As if on cue, the kitchen door swung open.

And in walked the one man who barely acknowledged her existence.

~

Vick Johnson paused in the doorway, sizing up the situation as all eyes turned toward him.

Kat and Jack greeted him with their usual warmth, but Lucy dropped her gaze to her coffee cup, hiding her face behind a sheet of honey-blond hair.

Just as well.

He didn't need the distraction of her intense blue eyes or her ever-present smile that put him on edge.

Focus on the mission.

"Hey, Jack. Can we talk for a sec?"

"Sure. But first, we need your opinion." Jack gestured toward the barstool beside Lucy, and Vick stiffened.

His instincts told him to retreat, but he couldn't leave without giving his official resignation.

Which wouldn't be easy.

He'd tried to quit his job at the diner months ago, but Jack had asked him to stay on until the inn was up and running. Although he was anxious to get on the road again, Vick agreed, knowing Jack had his hands full with the busy diner and handling the renovations of the inn.

Vick perched on the barstool, accidentally catching Lucy's eye.

She smiled, and nerves rippled through him like the first day of boot camp, an uncomfortable mix of apprehension and excitement.

Yep. He needed to clear out ASAP.

He'd made it a habit to never stay in one place more than a couple of years, but the urgency to move had never been this strong before. Poppy Creek had a way of tearing down the bunker he'd built around himself.

And Lucy…

Well, that was something else entirely.

"Here. Try this and tell me what you think." Jack slid a plate of flapjacks in front of him.

Aromatic steam curled from the pillowy crust, and Vick's stomach growled, reminding him that he hadn't eaten since his protein shake at 0600. And he'd run eight miles since then.

"Are you trying a new recipe?" He'd had Jack's famous flapjacks before, so he wasn't sure why his opinion was needed.

"Something like that." Jack tossed a playful wink in Kat's direction.

With an internal shrug, Vick dug his fork into the light, airy dough smothered in melted butter and thick maple syrup. He plopped it in his mouth, unnerved as they watched him chew.

The second he swallowed, Jack slapped his bearlike paw on the counter. "So, what'd you think?"

"It tastes as good as always. Or maybe a little better. Fluffier, I think."

Jack looked aghast as Kat whooped, throwing her fist in the air. Playful banter ensued, much to Vick's confusion.

Lucy leaned in close and whispered, "Uh-oh. You're in hot water now."

Her sultry, expensive-smelling perfume wafted toward him, and he resisted the urge to breathe deeply. "Why? What'd I miss?"

"Kat made the flapjacks," Lucy explained, biting back a laugh. "And I don't think Jack will ever forgive you for saying hers are better."

"Does that mean I'm fired?" Vick asked good-naturedly, though he secretly wondered if that would make things easier.

"Not a chance!" Jack bellowed jovially. "In fact, I have a favor to ask you."

Vick shifted on the barstool, suddenly on guard. Normally, he'd do just about anything for Jack. The guy was as good as they came, generous and big-hearted to a fault. Which was part of the problem. Over the past year, he'd become more than a boss. He'd become a friend. And Vick didn't have friends, as a general rule.

Vick braced himself, but Jack turned to Lucy instead. "Kat told me your latest YouTube video has over a million views."

"Over *two* million," Kat corrected. "Your little sister is becoming quite the celebrity."

Vick noticed a subtle blush creep up Lucy's neck, which surprised him. He assumed she'd be used to compliments.

"Not really." Lucy took a sip of coffee, deflecting behind the brim of her mug.

"Kat and I were talking," Jack continued, slinging his arm around Kat's shoulders. "And we were wondering if you could create a few videos about Poppy Creek, highlighting some of the fall happenings around here."

"The idea," Kat clarified, "is that by filming some of our fun events, people can see what makes Poppy Creek so special, and they'll want to visit and see what else the town has to offer. Which, of course, means they'll need a place to stay."

"That's not a bad idea." Lucy's forehead crinkled, and Vick could see her wheels turning. "I could add a link to the reservation portal beneath each video and give a shout-out at the end."

"That would be perfect!" Kat beamed.

"What events did you have in mind?" Lucy asked.

"Just the main ones," Jack told her. "The Apple Jubilee, Yarnfest, Pumpkins & Paws...."

"You could finish the video series with the Library Benefit Banquet," Kat added, her green eyes brightening.

Vick's pulse quickened, but he kept his composure, not wanting to give anything away. He intended to leave town that night. The fancy party at the inn would be the ideal opportunity to slip away without anyone noticing.

He wasn't big on goodbyes.

"Sounds like a plan." Lucy pulled out her phone and began typing notes to herself. "If my memory serves, there are six main events in the fall. I'll create a miniseries around them, take a couple of videos, intersperse them with a few still shots and descriptive text…."

Jack cleared his throat. "There's one other thing."

Vick's radar went off, sensing danger ahead.

"Going through your channel, we noticed your best performing videos have you in front of the camera, not behind it."

"That's true," Lucy admitted. "But I shoot those indoors with a tripod. If I'm filming events around town, I won't be able to be in the videos."

"Unless someone else records them, right?" A mischievous grin spread across Jack's rugged features.

"Are you volunteering? Because you can't even take a simple snapshot without cutting people's heads off," Lucy teased.

"Not me." Jack turned his gaze on Vick, whose flight instinct immediately kicked in.

"Me?" He wasn't exactly Steven Spielberg, either.

"Your résumé says you spent a year as an assistant to a wedding videographer in some small town in Sonoma County. Wasn't it your first job after you left the Marines?"

Vick suppressed a grimace. His hireability had hit rock bottom after his medical discharge, and an old buddy from basic training set him up with the gig to help him get back on his feet. He never thought it would lead to trouble.

"You know what?" Lucy blurted, her voice an octave higher than normal. "I could try using a GoPro or even a drone. Or maybe one of those selfie sticks?"

Vick cast her a sideways glance. He knew why *he* didn't want to work together, but what was her excuse?

"Vick doesn't mind," Jack said casually. "Do you, Vick?"

Vick swallowed, feeling backed into a corner and pinned down on all sides. "What about the diner?"

"I hired a new guy. He starts in a few days."

Vick's brain worked overtime to formulate a rebuttal, but

how could he say no without revealing his cards? He doubted Jack would appreciate the real reason he didn't want to spend time with his little sister. And all the excuses he could think of didn't sound much better than the truth.

He could feel everyone staring at him, and he realized he still hadn't given Jack an answer.

"Sure. I can help, I guess."

As Jack raved about how great it would be for business, Vick's stomach spun like the rotor on the Sikorsky Super Stallion helicopter.

Something told him he'd just agreed to an impossible mission.

And he'd be lucky if he made it out alive.

CHAPTER 2

Elbow-deep in soap suds, Lucy mulled over her escape plan as she helped Kat clean up from breakfast.

She wanted to tackle her brother for roping Vick into helping her. She'd spent months getting over her schoolgirl crush, and spending one-on-one time together might undo all her efforts.

Somehow, she'd have to get out of it.

Before she made a fool out of herself or worse… had her heart broken.

After rinsing the last plate, she handed it to Kat to dry.

"Thanks, Luce."

"No problem. I'm happy to help." Lucy dried her hands on a kitchen towel, barely listening as she pondered various excuses to get herself out of this mess.

"I don't mean the dishes." Kat's tone conveyed a seriousness that gave Lucy pause.

"Is everything okay?"

"I'm not sure." Kat sighed, and for the first time in months, some of the sparkle left her eyes.

"Here, sit down." Lucy ushered her toward the barstool, then refilled their coffee mugs before sitting beside her. "What's on your mind?"

Kat toyed with the curved handle, and Lucy noticed her nails had been gnawed to the tips of her fingers. "I'm a little embarrassed to admit this, but I'm nervous. Like, sometimes-I-can-barely-eat-or-sleep kind of nervous."

"I had no idea," Lucy breathed, her stomach twisting with empathy.

"I've tried to ignore it, but I can't help thinking about all the people who've put their faith in me. Especially Jack. What if I fail?"

"You won't." Lucy placed a hand on Kat's forearm and gave a reassuring squeeze. "I have no doubts, whatsoever."

"Thanks. I appreciate that." Kat smiled weakly. "But our timing for the grand opening isn't great. Tourism is always down in the fall and winter. At first, I thought that would be a good thing. That it would give us a chance to ease into a routine." She glanced down at her hands, nervously wound around the ceramic mug. "But what if we open all the rooms and I can't keep them filled?"

"What did Trudy say?" Lucy asked. No one would have better advice than Gertrude Hobbs. She and her husband, George, had owned the Morning Glory Inn for decades, and until recently, the small bed-and-breakfast was the only lodging option in Poppy Creek. The older woman had been acting as a mentor to Kat throughout the entire renovation and setup process.

"Trudy's been wonderful. A lifesaver, to be honest. She said I needed to be patient. And it takes time to get off the ground. I suppose I'm just being overly anxious. But I know how much everyone's invested in this place. Jack, you..." She met Lucy's gaze. "That's why I'm so grateful you agreed to do the videos. I know it won't be a magic bullet, but if you can inspire even a few people to make the trip, it will go a long way toward easing some of my nerves."

Lucy forced a smile.

Well, that settled it. She couldn't back out now.

"I'll do whatever I can to help, but I don't think you have anything to worry about."

Sisterly affection stole over Kat's features. "You're a lot like Jack, you know."

"You mean we're both blond-haired, blue-eyed versions of the Brawny Man?" Lucy teased. Her brother had often been compared to the muscular, flannel-clad mascot of the popular paper towel company. Although slightly outdated, the comparison was still pretty spot-on.

"No." Kat laughed. "But I'll have to remember that the next time he compares himself to Thor."

Lucy rolled her eyes. "He would."

"I was actually referring to what's on the inside," Kat said, her tone soft and sincere. "You both love others with your whole heart. And that's rare these days. Most of us hold back, afraid of getting hurt. But you don't. And that comes across in your videos, too. Which, I think, is part of the reason people are so drawn to you. Well, that and the obvious reasons," she added with a teasing grin.

Lucy blushed. She was used to people commenting on her appearance. To the point she sometimes wondered if that's all she had to offer. But Kat's compliment meant more to her than she could ever know. Although, it wasn't entirely deserved.

When it came to romantic love, she couldn't be more terrified.

"Hello?"

Startled, Lucy glanced over her shoulder. Her good friend Olivia Parker strolled into the kitchen carrying a festive arrangement of chrysanthemums and plum-colored roses. "I thought I might find you ladies in here."

"Liv! I wasn't expecting to see you today." Lucy slid off the barstool and waited for Olivia to set the vase on the counter before greeting her with a hug. "Shouldn't you be getting ready for the Apple Jubilee tomorrow?"

"Oh, I've been planning that for months. By now, it'll practically run itself." Olivia laughed.

Lucy didn't doubt it. Before she moved back to Poppy Creek, Olivia ran an elite event-planning service in New York, specializing in luxury celebrations and celebrity weddings.

When she reconnected with her childhood friend, Reed Hollis, last spring, Olivia purchased the orchard adjacent to his flower farm and they merged the two properties into the Sterling Rose Estate—Poppy Creek's premier event venue.

"Besides," Olivia added. "When Reed mentioned he'd be delivering the arrangements you ordered, I remembered I had a couple more ideas I wanted to run by you for the Library Benefit Banquet in a few weeks."

"I have to say," Kat gushed, burying her face in the fragrant petals, "your beau sure knows how to arrange a bouquet."

"Yes, he does." A pretty blush swept across Olivia's cheeks, and she self-consciously tucked a strand of dark hair behind her ear.

Lucy smiled, her heart bursting with happiness for her friend. Olivia had been through so much in the past year, between the devastating divorce and the loss of her business, it made Lucy a little teary-eyed to see her so content and blissful.

And yet, somewhere deep down—in a shadowy corner of her heart—a pang of jealousy lurked behind the joy.

But she wasn't sure what she envied more—the fact that both Kat and Olivia had partners to share their lives with or that they'd found their passions in life, something to give them drive and purpose.

Unbidden, her thoughts drifted to the business card buried in the bottom of her purse, and an unthinkable fear slithered into the back of her mind.

Even if she had both of those things, would it even matter anymore?

~

Leaning out the window of his Jeep, Vick pressed the pound sign on the keypad and waited for the long iron gate to swing open.

His landlord, Bill Tucker, owned a myriad of animals, from chickens to miniature goats to alpacas, and he let them all run loose on his farm, which made the gate a necessity.

Vick eased down the dirt road, being mindful of four-legged pedestrians.

Peggy Sue, a rotund, pot-belly pig with a fancy pink collar waddled across his path. Vick paused, idling until she made it to the other side, then continued toward the back of the spacious property.

While Bill treated all of his animals like beloved pets, Peggy Sue was undoubtedly his favorite, and she accompanied him everywhere.

At first, Vick found it strange, even somewhat worrisome. But when he learned Bill's late wife had weaned the pig from birth, he understood the sentimental attachment.

Shifting into park, he glanced at the eagle tattoo on his forearm. Most people assumed it had ties to his military service, and he never bothered to correct them. The true meaning wasn't anyone else's business.

Unwanted thoughts crept into the forefront of his mind, triggering a familiar tension in his chest. His breath quickened, and his lungs worked overtime.

Leaning against the headrest, he inhaled for a count of seven, then exhaled following the same pattern.

His heart continued to pound.

Unclenching his fist, he tapped his thumb against his pinky finger, then his ring finger, then middle, then pointer, repeating the process in a slow, methodical rhythm until his pulse returned to normal.

The first time the therapist taught him the calming technique, he'd scoffed, refusing to try it. Then, later that night, his nightmare returned, and he'd rocketed awake, dripping with sweat, his heart revolting against his rib cage.

Desperate for relief, he'd tossed aside his pride and tried the therapist's hokey trick. While it wasn't a miracle cure, his panic had eventually subsided.

The tension gone, Vick climbed out of the Jeep and strode toward his temporary home.

He'd agreed to rent it from Bill, sight unseen, but the second he laid eyes on the converted grain silo, he knew he'd made the right decision.

The quirky, cylindrical living space only had one bedroom and a half-bath with an enclosed shower out back, and the kitchen consisted of a microwave, mini fridge, and hot plate, but it suited his simple lifestyle. In fact, the glorified tin can had everything he needed, especially since he brought most of his food home from the diner. And when he cooked on his day off, he used the barbecue out on the patio.

Plus, it came with an unofficial—though somewhat ornery—roommate.

"Hey, Buddy." Vick knelt and extended his hand.

The miniature goat trotted toward him, nuzzling his palm with the top of his head.

"Sorry I missed breakfast this morning." Vick gave him a few scratches behind the ear. "But better late than never, right?"

That's when he noticed one of his boots by the front door—mangled within an inch of its life.

Vick sighed. Apparently, Buddy didn't agree with his better-late-than-never philosophy.

"Why is it always the expensive boots?" Vick asked, lifting the drool-covered footwear. "Why can't you destroy my ten-dollar sandals instead?"

He glanced at Buddy, whose black and gray markings gave the appearance of a perpetual smile.

"Oh, you think it's funny, do you? We'll see if I share my apple with you now."

Even as he pushed through the front door and tossed the boot in the garbage, he knew he wouldn't make good on the threat.

Buddy must've known, too, because he pranced around the kitchen while Vick brewed a fresh pot of coffee.

Most mornings, he woke up at 0600, went for a run, then sat with Buddy on the front porch, sipping coffee and sharing apple slices.

Today, he'd been anxious to talk to Jack, so he'd skipped their ritual and headed straight for the inn.

Clearly, Buddy hadn't appreciated the change in plans.

Steaming cup of coffee in hand, Vick settled in the rickety rocking chair with a view of the bucolic farm.

Buddy waited by his feet, his dark eyes locked on the apple in Vick's grasp.

"First, apologize for ruining my shoe," Vick said in as stern a tone as he could muster.

The little goat placed his chin on Vick's knee, his tiny nub of a tail wiggling.

"All right, apology accepted." Vick chuckled, flipping open his tactical knife. He cut a generous slice and tossed it to Buddy.

The impish goat gobbled it down.

Vick usually spent his days off helping Bill around the farm. But today, he had an important task to check off the list.

After they finished the apple, Vick overturned an old milk crate and spread out a worn map of the United States.

Red circles marked all the places he'd lived since leaving the Marines.

So far, he'd stuck to small towns but had noticed a troubling pattern. The friendly townspeople inevitably tried to corral him into their close-knit communities. He needed a larger city, somewhere he could blend in and keep to himself.

An image of his mother flashed into his mind, dragging his thoughts back in time.

He could still smell the rancid leftovers and pungent liquor bottles abandoned in the dumpster directly below their apartment window. Sirens wailed in the distance. A baby cried in the unit next door.

"One of these days, we'll live in a place like this." His mother had unfolded a glossy brochure for a small mountain community up north, gazing fondly at the idyllic photos of a family boating on the lake, roasting marshmallows around a campfire, and enjoying funnel cake at a county fair.

Despite being abandoned at nineteen by her husband of one year, left to raise an infant on her own, and working multiple jobs to make ends meet, his mother had managed to keep her sense of optimism.

Right up until the day she died.

A loud *rip* yanked Vick back to the present.

Buddy munched on a mouthful of map with an unsurprising air of nonchalance.

"Buddy," Vick groaned, assessing the damage.

A huge chunk of Alaskan wilderness now resided in Buddy's stomach, but the mischievous scamp had sparked an idea.

There was just one obstacle standing in the way.

His ties to Poppy Creek were a lot stronger than he wanted to admit.

CHAPTER 3

Brimming with excitement, Lucy gazed in awe at the bustling festivities of the Apple Jubilee.

Olivia had really outdone herself this time.

Brightly colored banners and bunting stretched above the sprawling lawn at the Sterling Rose Estate. Townspeople mingled around booths selling everything from jars of applesauce in every flavor imaginable—including jalapeño and spicy sriracha—and canned apple pie filling with gift tags proclaiming *Crust Optional.* Off to the side, a gaggle of giggling children swarmed around a cornucopia of carnival games, filling the crisp fall air with the sounds of youthful merriment.

The only thing spoiling the magical ambiance was Vick's lackluster attitude. He'd barely said two words since they arrived, and his stiff body language indicated he couldn't wait to be done with the assignment.

But Lucy wouldn't let his bad mood ruin her good time.

"Let's start with Sadie's booth." She maneuvered around a group of laughing teens bobbing for apples, heading toward a cluster of tables beneath a shady maple tree.

Sadie Hamilton, the owner of Poppy Creek's quintessential

candy store, stood behind an adorably decorated booth serving hot apple cider topped with whipped cream and a drizzle of caramel sauce.

To the right of her booth, event goers gathered around a long farm table dipping their own candied apples.

"You made it!" Sadie paused in the middle of refilling her tray of complimentary apple cider doughnuts.

"I wouldn't miss it. Plus, Jack asked us to film a few promotional videos of the festival. I'd love to feature your booth, if you don't mind."

"Not at all. But if you want to make candied apples, you have to pick your own."

"Really?" Vick frowned, clearly not grasping the charm of the experience.

"Yep. Those are the rules." Sadie grinned brightly, either missing his grumpy tone or choosing to ignore it.

Knowing Sadie, Lucy guessed it was the latter. "Point us in the right direction."

Sadie handed her a wicker basket and gestured toward a narrow path leading to the orchard. "Right through there."

Lucy led the way, suppressing a laugh when Sadie called out to their retreating backs, "Have fun!" and Vick mumbled something unintelligible under his breath.

Someone must have woken up on the wrong side of the bed—or continent. Fortunately, she had enough enthusiasm for both of them.

"Don't you love the smell of fall? It has this slightly sweet and musky scent."

"That's the decaying leaves," Vick explained, once again missing the point. "As the organic matter breaks down, it releases a distinct odor."

"How lovely." Lucy rolled her eyes, stopping at a tall wooden ladder. "Why don't I climb up and toss the apples down to you? We can make a game of it." She was determined to get at least one smile out of him.

Skeptical, he raised an eyebrow. "No offense, but if we have to eat these apples, I'd rather not."

"Are you doubting my aim?"

He lifted his shoulders in a noncommittal shrug.

She suppressed a smirk. Growing up with five older brothers meant she had to hone her athletic skills quickly if she wanted to be included in their shenanigans.

Unraveling her Burberry scarf, she arranged it in the bottom of the basket.

"What's that for?" Vick asked.

"To cushion the impact. I'm going to toss you a perfect apple, then challenge you to find a single bruise on it. If you can't, I get to make your caramel apple, which you have to eat without a single complaint."

"Challenge accepted." His dark eyes glinted. "Should we record it for posterity?"

"Good idea. That way, you can't deny my victory."

The corner of his lips twitched ever so slightly. Not quite a smile, but she was getting close to cracking him.

She mounted the ladder, climbing all the way to the top rung.

"Feeling cocky, are we?" Vick shouted from below.

"Not cocky, *confident*." She reached for a plump apple that gleamed a stunning shade of red and plucked it from the branch. Not a single nick or worm hole to be seen.

"Ready?" Vick pointed the camera through the branches.

Lucy glanced down, eyeing the basket by his feet. It looked much farther away at second glance.

For a brief moment, she wavered.

What if she missed?

~

Through the camera lens, Vick zoomed in on Lucy's expression, catching a flicker of hesitation in her eyes.

His stomach swirled at the increased intimacy of observing her so closely, catching him off guard.

He swallowed, his throat suddenly dry, and quickly zoomed out.

"I'm ready," she called down, sounding more self-assured than she looked.

Adjusting her stance on the ladder, she chose an underhand approach.

She pursed her lips, cocking them to the side in concentration as she lobbed the apple in his direction with one smooth motion.

He held his breath, following its trajectory.

The second it made contact with the bottom of the basket, Lucy whooped in triumph.

Angling the camera back on her face, he captured the way her eyes sparkled and the subtle crinkle of her nose.

Momentarily transfixed, he couldn't look away even if he wanted to.

She exuded a palpable joy, a radiance unlike anything he'd ever seen before. And she made it look effortless.

He chalked it up to the privilege of someone who'd never seen the ugliness of the world before. She embodied innocence, unscathed by tragedy or hardship.

"I hope you like your caramel apples dipped in red hots and sour gummies," she teased, hopping off the last rung of the ladder.

Snapping out of his trance, he shut off the camera, replacing the lens cap. "If you're making mine, does that mean I get to make yours?"

"Sure," she relented after a moment's consideration. "But because I won, I get to pick the toppings. And I want a *lot* of pink sprinkles."

He groaned, regretting his suggestion.

Lucy laughed, and the sound wrapped around him like a thick flannel blanket—warm and comforting. Why did she have that effect on him?

On paper, she wasn't his type. Young, naive, too flighty for her own good. She seemed to wander through life on a whim with zero drive or ambition. Plus, they had absolutely nothing in common.

And yet, she had an intangible, luminous quality he couldn't explain. Although, it certainly wasn't unappealing.

He shook his head, dismissing the uncomfortable thought as he followed her up the path to rejoin the festivities.

"Do you smell that?" She sniffed the air like a military canine detecting explosives.

"You mean moldy leaves again?" He couldn't help a grin.

"More like cinnamon and sugar, smart guy." She flashed an infectious smile, then wove through the crowd on a mission to uncover the source, momentarily putting their candy apple making on pause.

Along the way, they stopped to record a short video of an impressive apple juggler, followed by a surprisingly suspenseful apple-pressing contest to see who could fill a gallon jug the quickest.

The whole event couldn't have been quirkier, and he kept thinking about how much his mother would've loved it, in all its bizarre glory.

"Aha! We found it!" Lucy tugged on his sleeve, drawing his attention to a hand-painted sign for Old-Fashioned Fried Apple Pies.

Eliza Carter, the head baker at The Calendar Café, stood at a makeshift cooking station, tending to a sizzling iron skillet. The mouthwatering aroma of caramelized sugar and fragrant spices wafted toward them.

Eliza's young son, Ben, managed the cash box with the help of a scruffy gray terrier on guard by his feet. "We have classic apple and apple cranberry," Ben recited the flavors in a grown-up, professional tone as he pushed his glasses up the bridge of his nose. "All donations are for new art supplies at school." Breaking character, he beamed proudly, adding in a hushed voice, "Mom let me pick where the money went."

"Excellent choice." Lucy nodded her approval. "We'll take two classics, please."

Vick reached into his back pocket for his wallet, but Lucy beat him to it.

She handed Ben a fifty-dollar bill, telling him to keep the change without batting an eyelash.

While he admired her generosity, Vick doubted she'd ever had to worry about money a day in her life, and added it to their long list of irreconcilable differences.

Pies in hand, they meandered through the throng, taking in the celebratory sights and sounds.

Somewhere in the distance, someone called all contestants competing in the apple-tasting contest to meet at the yellow tent, where they'd be blindfolded and asked to guess the apple variety based on a single slice.

Vick shook his head in amusement before taking his first bite of pie. The buttery crust melted in his mouth, revealing a syrupy filling with just the right combination of sweetness and hint of tart.

"What do you think?" Lucy asked.

"One of the best things I've ever tasted," he answered honestly.

"Jack and I used to make these to sell on the street corner, only we called them hand pies and sold blackberry and cherry, too." Her features softened into a faraway smile as though reliving the nostalgic memory. "It was our version of a lemonade stand. Jack did all the baking, and I handled the sales."

Vick imagined she could sell Red Sox memorabilia to a Yankees fan. "Why'd you sell them? As a pastime?"

It wasn't like she needed the money. Her family owned half of Primrose Valley, and parts of Poppy Creek, too.

"Mostly to raise money for the book fair. I had my eye on an *Anne of Green Gables* box set."

"Your parents didn't give you money for the book fair?" he asked without thinking.

Too late, he realized the rudeness of his surprised tone, not to mention the general impropriety of his question.

But she didn't seem fazed by it.

"Oh, they would've if they could. But for some misguided reason, they thought putting food on the table was more important than new books." She laughed, and Vick gaped, beyond dumbfounded.

His disbelief quickly evolved into disappointment at his biased assumptions. It had never occurred to him that Lucy's family didn't always have money.

And he couldn't help wondering how else he'd misjudged her.

CHAPTER 4

Lucy fluffed the fragrant flower arrangement, barely noticing the unusual aubergine hue of the rose petals or their stunning golden tips. She couldn't stop thinking about the Apple Jubilee a few days ago. Or more specifically, how much fun she'd had with Vick once he'd loosened up.

What had made him so guarded? Was it his time in the Marines or something else? She fantasized about asking him and the even more implausible scenario of him actually giving her a transparent answer.

During her musings, a haziness crept into her thoughts, settling in the back of her mind. Suddenly disoriented and foggy-headed, she tried to refocus on the task at hand.

Their first guest, Jayla Moore, would be arriving today. She was a referral from Kat's mother figure, Fern Flores, who ran a women's shelter in Starcross Cove.

Kat wanted to place Jayla in the Zephyr Suite, their most luxurious accommodation with a spacious en suite bathroom and private balcony overlooking the garden.

Lucy loved the room and had gone to extra lengths to track down just the right oriental rug, matching Windsor chairs with rich, eye-catching upholstery to place in front of the marble fireplace, and the most sumptuous drapes to accent the tall windows and French doors. The antique Chippendale secretary desk was her favorite find, and the flowers looked lovely perched on top.

The vibrant colors of the bouquet momentarily blurred together, and Lucy blinked a few times, relieved when her vision returned to normal.

Must've been a false alarm.

Moving through her checklist, she adjusted the plate of cookies beside the welcome basket. Each sugary treat resembled an autumn leaf, decorated in various colors of intricately applied frosting, courtesy of The Calendar Café.

Shortly after Jayla's arrival, Kat would bring up a silver coffee service with the café's special Southern Pecan blend to accompany the delicate desserts.

Everything had been carefully thought out, down to the smallest detail.

Lucy gave a sharp shake of her head, distracted by a faint humming in her ears. After a moment, she realized her phone was vibrating in her back pocket.

"Hi, Mom."

"Lucy, my love. How are you, darling?"

"Same as yesterday." For the last few weeks, her mother had called nearly every day with some new scheme to convince Lucy to come home.

Although she repeatedly refused, Elaine Gardener was nothing if not persistent.

"Have you given any more thought to my proposal?"

With a heavy sigh, Lucy tucked the phone between her chin and shoulder to fluff the embroidered throw pillows on the four-poster bed. "Thanks for the offer, but I'm not interested in being the secretary for the Ladies of the Valley."

Her mother had been pressuring her to join the fancy women's society for several years. And although they did some good things—like organizing fundraisers—it more closely resembled a cloister of socialites who liked to gossip and hold high tea.

"One of these days, I'll convince you," Elaine said with a lighthearted laugh, clearly undeterred. "Did I tell you Lois's son, Brennan, is back in town?"

"Yes. Several times." The humming noise grew to a rhythmic throbbing.

Lucy's pulse quickened.

Please, not again....

She closed her eyes, as though she could halt a runaway train with sheer willpower.

"Oh, well, I couldn't remember," Elaine said casually, "and since you haven't mentioned getting together with him, I thought perhaps I'd forgotten to tell you."

Lucy leaned against the bed, a wave of nausea washing over her. "Mom, I have to go." Surplus saliva slicked the back of her throat, and she swallowed, desperate to stave off what inevitably came next.

"Don't be so dramatic, darling. Going on a date with Brennan Hollingsworth would be good for you. He has a great job, and he's actually quite handsome now. Reminds me of a young George Clooney. Do girls your age even know who George Clooney is anymore?"

Her mother laughed again, but the normally pleasant sound reverberated in Lucy's ears like a high-pitched smoke alarm—piercing and painful.

The pressure between her temples increased until she feared her skull might collapse from the force. She sank to her knees, the phone slipping from her hand, clattering against the floor.

She still heard her mother's muffled voice through the speaker, but she couldn't make out what she was saying.

Cradling her head, Lucy curled into a ball, whimpering helplessly as she waited for the pain to pass.

As it had all the times before.

~

Vick unlocked the front door to the diner, then glanced over his shoulder.

Still no sign of the new guy.

Hadn't Colt told him to meet the new line cook at 0900?

He checked the time on his phone. It was only five minutes past, he should probably cut the guy some slack on his first day. Besides, Colt Davis wasn't the most reliable when it came to relaying messages. He could've gotten the time wrong. Between working a few hours at the diner, opening the new restaurant at the inn, and helping Frank Barrie roast coffee part-time, Vick would be surprised if the man ever slept.

Not to mention, he was still technically a newlywed.

Vick directed his gaze toward the bright-teal door of Thistle & Thorn, the antiques shop owned by Colt's wife, Penny. She often came by the diner for lunch or simply to stop in and say hi to Colt. Their affection for each other bordered on nauseating at times. Which was especially surprising since Colt was the last person on earth Vick expected to settle down.

Well, besides himself.

For the last year, he'd witnessed countless couples throw caution to the wind, like a grenade without a safety pin.

And he hated the thought that each of their fledgling relationships might blow up in their unsuspecting faces.

But if life had taught him anything, it was that some things—like heartache—were painfully inevitable.

"Sorry I'm late."

The winded voice tugged Vick from his thoughts.

As he focused on the approaching figure, he did a double take.

The man hurrying across the street toward him was at least two decades older than he'd expected. A smattering of silvery-gray strands speckled his sandy-colored hair, which could stand a decent trim. Creases around his eyes and mouth gave character to his tanned, ruggedly handsome features. And although he was twice his age, Vick had to hand it to the guy—he clearly worked out.

"No problem." Vick offered his hand. "I'm Vick. Vick Johnson. You're technically my replacement, so I'll be showing you how I normally prep for the lunch crowd. Jack should be along in an hour or so."

"Rhett Douglas. Great to meet you."

Vick appreciated his strong handshake, but there was something unusual—almost intrusive—in the man's gaze.

"So, Rhett, where are you from?" He pushed through the front door, letting it swing shut behind them.

Rhett hesitated before answering, "The central valley, north of Bakersfield."

"Ah, all good things come from Bakersfield." Vick chuckled, momentarily forgetting who he was talking to.

Rhett shot him a puzzled expression.

Embarrassed, Vick furnished a half-cocked grin. "Sorry. That's something my mom used to say. She was born there, and her mother before that, and so on for five generations."

"Is that where you were born?"

"No. My mom moved to Los Angeles the second she turned eighteen. Said she wanted to be the next Julia Roberts."

He neglected to add how she'd married a lowlife who'd knocked her up then split when he couldn't handle the responsibility.

Vick waited for Rhett to ask if his mother ever made it in showbiz, but he never did. Maybe he could hear the bleakness in his voice.

Switching gears, Vick gave him a tour of the diner with a breakdown of the company culture and job expectations.

Rhett seemed especially appreciative that they only opened for lunch and dinner, which meant no early-morning shifts.

As they chopped vegetables in preparation for lunch service,

Vick asked, "What brings you to Poppy Creek? Do you have family in town?"

Rhett diced onions with the speed and precision of someone who'd done it a thousand times before. Between his glazed eyes and clenched jaw, Vick wondered if he'd struck a nerve, but chalked it up to the onion fumes.

After a beat, Rhett said, "I wanted a change in pace. And Poppy Creek seems like a great community."

"It is," he answered sincerely.

And as he worked side by side with his replacement, he felt an unexpected twinge of hesitation.

As if, somewhere deep down, he wasn't as anxious to leave as he should be.

CHAPTER 5

"Have you seen Lucy?" Vick asked, approaching Kat at the reservation desk.

She tapped a finger to her chin. "Now that you mention it, I haven't seen her for a few hours. Not since she went upstairs this morning to put a few finishing touches on the Zephyr Suite. Our first guest is arriving today."

"Congratulations." He managed a small smile despite the nerves plaguing him all morning.

He'd thought of a few excuses to get out of today's event but couldn't bring himself to pull the trigger. "We were supposed to meet out front before heading to Yarnfest."

"Why don't you check upstairs? And would you mind setting this in the welcome basket while you're there?" She handed him a box of chocolates from Sadie's Sweet Shop.

"Will do." He headed toward the staircase, half hoping Lucy had forgotten about today. The knowledge that he might have misjudged her only added to his apprehension about spending time together. He already found her dangerously attractive. What if all his previous objections had no basis in reality?

Since he'd sworn off dating, he needed the consolation of their irredeemable differences to maintain a safe distance.

Halfway down the hall, he spotted Lucy emerge from the Zephyr Suite.

Something immediately seemed odd about her stride, and as she drew nearer, he noticed a distinct pallor to her complexion.

"Are you okay?"

"Yeah, why?" She ran her fingers through her hair, smoothing down the flyaways.

Were her fingers trembling? He used to see similar symptoms during field exercises when recruits skipped meals to make their weight.

"You look pale. Have you eaten anything today?"

"No, I haven't. That must be it." Her rushed answer triggered suspicion.

Would hunger explain the strained squint of her eyes? Or the smear of mascara around the edges, as if she'd been crying.

"Are you sure you're okay?"

"Uh-huh." She swiped at the smudges, forcing a smile.

But he wasn't convinced. "I have to drop this off in the suite, then let's grab something quick to eat from the kitchen before we leave. And I'll drive this time."

She didn't argue, which surprised him. Even more strange, she sat silently in the passenger seat for most of the trek into town, alternating between sips from her water bottle and nibbling on a plain slice of toast.

On high alert, he stole frequent sideways glances, trying to gauge whether or not to voice his concern.

Fortunately, by the time they parked and joined the hustle and bustle in the town square, her spirits had lifted and most of the color had returned to her cheeks.

Although, something still seemed off.

He decided to keep a watchful eye on her as they toured the booths, just in case something shifted again.

As far as Vick could tell, Yarnfest was a humongous artisan fair featuring textile arts and crafts with added quirks in true Poppy Creek fashion.

Most of the activities were centralized in the spacious town square, but the Western-style storefronts lining all four streets were adorned with woven signs featuring festive puns like Paid in Wool, and I've Got a Knotty Habit.

Across the lawn, he spotted Bill Tucker and two of his alpacas, Perry and Como, near a stand selling scarves made out of their spun wool.

Vick waved, but Bill was too busy keeping Perry from spitting on an unsuspecting tourist.

On their way to view an antique loom from the 1800s, they passed a knitting contest where several women—and one burly man with an intricately braided beard—wielded long needles with lightning speed, attempting to complete a round potholder before the others.

Behind the camera lens, Lucy's lack of energy was even more apparent. She smiled and said all the right things, but she'd lost the light in her eyes.

As soon as they got enough footage, he replaced the lens cap and slipped the strap from around his neck. "I'll be right back." He trotted toward his Jeep and tucked the camera in the footwell.

For a split second, it occurred to him that he had the perfect excuse to take off. They'd finished their mission. He didn't need to stay. He could tell Lucy goodbye and be done with it.

Wavering, he glanced over his shoulder.

Lucy perused a display of cashmere gloves, keeping to herself. Normally, she'd be chatting up the artisan, charming them with her gregarious smile and engaging sense of humor.

With a decisive stride, Vick rejoined her in the square and gently placed a hand on the small of her back.

Big mistake.

An unexpected current surged up his arm, and he yanked his palm away, startled by the sensation.

She met his gaze, a questioning glint in her eyes.

He cleared his throat. "There's something over here I thought we should check out."

Ignoring the heat snaking across his chest, he led her to a stand selling something called Bird's Nest Baklava.

The interesting-looking dessert did indeed resemble a mini bird's nest, crafted from sinewy strips of dough threaded together with a cluster of honey-glazed pistachios in the center.

Visually, each bite-size morsel was a work of art. And perfectly matched the quirky theme of Yarnfest.

"Hi, you two." Beverly Barrie greeted them with a warm smile that creased the corners of her pale periwinkle-blue eyes.

From the moment he met the head librarian, Vick liked her. On the outside, she looked prim and proper with her endless wardrobe of pastel cardigans and white hair coiled in an elegant bun. But he'd never met anyone more knowledgeable about epic Westerns and military sci-fi. And since arriving in Poppy Creek, he hadn't checked out a single library book he didn't enjoy, thanks to her recommendations.

He still found it hard to believe the winsome, soft-spoken woman had married Frank Barrie, the legendary town hermit who'd only recently rejoined society. The man's brusque demeanor and rusty social skills could be off-putting, to say the least.

Not that he couldn't relate.

After a few minutes of chitchat, Beverly handed them a plate of baklava with a brief explanation of the unique treat and its tie to Frank's Armenian heritage.

A heavy weight settled in Vick's stomach whenever someone spoke about their culture or background.

Since his father left before he was born, and his mother never talked about him, Vick always felt like half of his identity was missing. Which only magnified his state of isolation, even before he lost everyone who had ever mattered to him.

Beverly handed Lucy a second plate and nodded toward a neighboring booth. "Would you mind taking this over to Frank? He's been helping Cassie serve coffee at the donation drop-off all morning, and he's starting to get the *look*." She pursed her lips, giving her best sour-faced expression. "Something sweet will help stave off the surliness, which I know we'll all appreciate." She laughed, light and delicate. The sound had the same melodic quality of his mother's laugh, like a songbird welcoming the sunrise.

At the thought of his mother, bitter remorse rose like bile in his throat.

Why hadn't she told him about her illness? Maybe he could've done something. Or at least helped her through it.

Instead, she'd been ripped from his life without him even knowing anything was wrong.

And he wasn't sure he could ever forgive her for that… no matter her reasons.

~

Lucy popped the bite-size baklava into her mouth, savoring the surprising crunch and syrupy sweetness of the honey.

She almost hadn't come today, unsure if she'd be able to handle the noise and commotion since the aftermath of her migraines could last anywhere from a few hours to a few days. About a month ago, they'd sprang out of nowhere, occurring once a week or so. After the first two or three, she'd finally made an appointment to see Dr. Dunlap, who appeared concerned at their sudden and unexplainable development. It also didn't help that her symptoms were inconsistent, varying in severity from one episode to the next.

At least this time, the lingering effects had already started to dissipate, making it possible for her to fulfill her promise. She couldn't let Kat down. Especially since the first video seemed to be working.

After she'd edited and posted the footage from the Apple Jubilee, she didn't check on it for a few days, keeping her expectations low. But Kat had phoned early that morning, raving about a new booking for next week and a couple who'd reserved ten whole days next fall for their anniversary, citing the video.

Kat's excitement had been palpable through the speakers, and she continued to effuse her thanks when Lucy arrived at the inn a few hours later. How could she back out when she knew how much it meant to her?

Luckily, the food and water—and remarkably, Vick's company—served to alleviate some of the symptoms. Hopefully, the caffeine-rich coffee at Cassie and Frank's booth would also help.

"Lucy! Just the woman I wanted to see." Cassie's exuberant smile encapsulated every part of her being, from her relaxed, welcoming posture to the unmistakable shimmer in her deep-green eyes.

"Hey, Cass." Lucy felt the last bit of tension slip from her neck and shoulders.

Although they'd met only a few months ago, Cassie Davis had a way of making each person feel like the center of the universe, like she genuinely cared about the nuances of their life. And Lucy had quickly counted her among her closest friends.

"Jack dropped off your donations earlier. Well, he didn't *say* they were yours, but the Chanel cashmere sweaters were easy to distinguish from the array of flannel shirts." She laughed, shaking her head in amusement, then her features softened. "All those items you donated were incredibly generous. And I wanted to thank you in person."

Lucy sensed Vick's eyes on her, and she prayed the color of

her cheeks didn't match their heat level. "Not necessary. I was happy to do it."

Reading her discomfort, Cassie didn't say anything more about it, busying herself with pouring two cups of aromatic coffee.

Lucy's heart warmed at the way Cassie hummed softly while she worked, speaking to the level of happiness over the day's event.

The donations of blankets and clothing were for a cause dear to Cassie's heart—a veterans homeless shelter in San Francisco that Frank Barrie had secretly supported for years.

When Cassie found out, she took it a step further and crafted a new coffee to serve at The Calendar Café, and sell on their website, all proceeds benefiting the shelter. She called it the Freedom Blend—a bold brew to support the brave.

Once again, Lucy couldn't help noticing how everyone around her had found the intersection between their passion, talent, and purpose. And they made it look so easy and uncomplicated.

"Is this the Freedom Blend?" Lucy asked, lifting the cup to her lips. The heady aroma of tart berries and rich chocolate tickled her nose.

"No, this is a new one Colt came up with this morning." Some of the brightness faded from Cassie's eyes. "We're really going to miss him once the restaurant at the inn opens full-time."

Her gaze wandered to Frank at the other end of the booth, who'd been cornered by Frida Connelly. The older woman appeared to be giving Frank a long list of care instructions for the quilt she'd donated.

Cassie didn't elaborate on her concerns, but she didn't have to—Lucy had overheard Colt discussing it with Kat the other day. He felt guilty for abandoning Frank, knowing Cassie couldn't spare any more time from the café. And with Frank's age and recent health scare, he couldn't do all the roasting on his own anymore. Which created a conundrum for them all.

Engrossed in her conversation with Cassie, Lucy hadn't noticed Vick retrieve the camera from the Jeep until she heard the whir of the shutter.

He snapped a handful of shots featuring the booth, and asked Cassie if he could record a brief video while she talked about the shelter.

Behind the camera, Vick's features softened, a blend of appreciation and something darker—pain, sorrow, remorse? She wasn't sure. But it was apparent how deeply he cared about the cause.

Although he was stoic and reserved on the outside, she suspected a wellspring of emotion hid beneath the surface.

And if she wasn't careful, her schoolgirl crush could turn into something much deeper… and far more devastating.

CHAPTER 6

As they drove back to the inn, Vick replayed the video he'd taken of Cassie over in his mind. While he appreciated the work of the shelter, he hated that such places were necessary. Too many men and women came back from the war without the resources and help they needed. In cases of substance abuse among veterans, many could be traced back to undiagnosed post-traumatic stress. The shame surrounding the disorder didn't help, either, since service members often avoided testing.

In his case, he wasn't given a choice.

His fingers clenched around the steering wheel, tension traveling up his forearms.

He caught Lucy staring and loosened his grip, but it was too late.

She must've put two and two together because she asked, "How long were you in the Marines?"

"Two tours in Afghanistan." He adjusted his hands, airing out his sweaty palms.

Even with the windows cracked, and the cool breeze filtering through the crevice, the air inside the Jeep grew uncomfortably warm.

"What made you leave the military?"

At her question, a muscle in his jaw involuntarily flexed. When asked, he usually avoided giving an answer, deftly changing the subject.

"If you don't want to talk about it, I completely understand." Something in her tone shifted, revealing a care and thoughtfulness he hadn't expected.

Most people asked him about his service with a note of morbid curiosity or inconsiderate self-interest, as though he owed them entertainment value along with their hard-fought freedom.

Remarkably, he found himself formulating an honest response. "I left on medical discharge. It wasn't by choice."

"Oh, Vick." She breathed his name with so much concern, his own throat tightened. "Are you okay?"

Her gaze combed over his body, as if searching for a visible injury despite the coverage of his blue jeans and lightweight bomber jacket.

Funny how people always assumed wounds were physical.

Under her scrutiny, he shifted in his seat. "I'm fine." His voice sounded strangely husky, and he was grateful they'd arrived at the inn.

He hopped out of the driver's seat and opened her door, which had an annoying habit of getting stuck.

She slipped to the ground and met his gaze, hesitating as if she had something else to say.

At just over six feet, he had only two inches on her, which put her face dangerously close to his.

He noticed the subtle way she drew her bottom lip between her teeth, kneading it nervously. She gathered a breath, and surprised him by saying, "See you in a few days for the Readathon," before scurrying toward the front steps.

Torn, he watched her disappear through the double doors in a blur of blond hair and the fluttering fringe of her plaid scarf.

The more time they spent together, the more conflicted he felt each time they parted ways.

He thought about the job application sitting on his computer at home.

It was filled out, he simply needed to press Send.

But something kept holding him back.

~

By the time Lucy entered the foyer, her pulse pounded inside her chest.

Collecting herself, she leaned against the doorframe.

She was falling for Vick. *Hard.*

And she needed to snap out of it.

The more she got to know him, the further she fell.

But now wasn't the time to start a relationship, even if Vick was amenable to the idea.

Her last migraine had been worse than the others, and she wasn't sure what that meant. Would they keep escalating?

The business card for the specialist had been burning a hole in the bottom drawer of her nightstand for the last several days, but she couldn't bring herself to dial the number.

She hated the uncertainty surrounding the cause of her migraines, but a definitive answer might be even worse.

There was a glimmer of hope in not knowing.

Especially since one of the possible causes overwhelmed her with fear.

Her thoughts drifted to Vick's medical discharge from the military, and a heavy weight pressed on her heart. What had happened to him? Was he really all right?

There was so much she didn't know. And he didn't seem keen on telling her.

"Lucy!" Kat called from across the room.

Summoning a smile, Lucy approached the reservation desk where Kat was checking in a young woman roughly her own age.

"I'd like you to meet Jayla Moore," Kat said. "Jayla, this is Lucy Gardener. She's our interior designer. All the incredible details you'll see throughout your stay are thanks to her talent and vision."

"It's a pleasure to meet you." Jayla offered her hand. Against her stunning dark brown complexion, Lucy noticed heavy circles under her eyes, hinting at fatigue.

"We're so happy you're our first guest," Lucy said sincerely, already eager to get to know her better.

"Jayla is an American Sign Language specialist." Kat spoke with an air of admiration. "She works specifically with women and children in shelters, teaching them ASL and interpreting for them. She travels all over the country offering her special skill."

Jayla waved aside Kat's praise, adding humbly, "It's not as selfless as it sounds. I love what I do."

Lucy studied her with fresh eyes. To think, at such a young age, she was already doing such important work.

Kat handed her a brass key tied to a silver cord. "You're in the Zephyr Suite. Once you're settled, would you like me to bring up a tea or coffee service?"

"Actually, after the long drive, I was hoping to stretch my legs. Are there any short walking trails you'd recommend?"

"There are several excellent trails around town." Kat slid open a drawer and removed a rudimentary map. "But my favorite spot is right in our backyard." With a pencil, she traced a path through the gardens, leading into the thicket. "Half a mile into the woods, you'll see a small clearing, surrounded on all sides by towering sycamore trees. There, you'll find a bench. You'll want to sit directly in the center."

Jayla raised an eyebrow, her interest piqued. "And why is that?"

Kat merely smiled. "When you get there, you'll see. For now, let's just say it has a knack for alleviating tired travelers and troubled thoughts."

Jayla didn't look convinced, but she folded the map and stuffed it into her purse.

Lucy couldn't help thinking she should take the walk herself sometime soon.

Kat told Jayla about a few more trails before directing her toward her room. She waited for her to disappear up the winding staircase before gushing, "I'm so glad she's staying with us! Fern adores her. She's been helping a woman at Hope Hideaway whose ten-year-old daughter is deaf."

"Wow," Lucy murmured, still struggling with the idea of a child living in a women's shelter.

"So, how was Yarnfest?" Kat asked, switching gears entirely.

"Um, it was fun." Lucy's thoughts lingered on Jayla and the work she was doing across the country.

"Did Vick come back with you?"

"No, he dropped me off. He's working at the diner tonight."

"Jack is really going to miss him. Well, we all will."

"What do you mean?" Lucy straightened, Kat's comment capturing her full attention.

"He turned in his resignation. I don't know if he plans to stay past the end of the month. I'm sorry, Luce, I thought you knew."

Lucy pressed a hand to the counter to steady herself.

Vick was leaving? And so soon?

She wasn't sure why the news hit her so hard. It wasn't as if she'd planned to stay in Poppy Creek forever, either.

In fact, now that the inn was up and running, her interior design skills were no longer needed.

And yet, the reality of them both moving on with their lives hadn't really sunk in… until now.

Why hadn't Vick told her?

CHAPTER 7

Vick scooped a hefty portion of their famous Garlic Gold Rush fries onto the plate beside the Boom Town Burger and slid it across the counter for the server.

With Jack out front seating customers and managing the bar —where he served his specialty sarsaparilla floats—Vick and Colt were left to run the kitchen.

Things always ran more smoothly when Jack and Colt worked separately, since they butted heads over the menu on a constant basis. Jack liked to keep things simple and classic, while Colt had a habit of making creative tweaks and adding spur-of-the-moment garnishes that didn't always go over well—the pickled beets on the bacon cheeseburger readily came to mind. Although, his culinary skills couldn't be denied, which is why Jack asked him to manage the restaurant at the inn.

Between Colt's new role and Vick leaving town in a few weeks, the diner staff was dwindling. He hoped the new guy stuck around awhile.

As if reading his mind, Colt asked, "What d'you think of the new guy?"

"I like him. Kinda intense, but he knows his stuff. And what he doesn't know, he picks up quickly."

"I should poach him to work at the inn. I wouldn't even have to bribe him, just tell him he'd be working for me instead of Jack." Colt flashed his trademark dimpled grin.

Chuckling, Vick gave a rueful shake of his head.

Apparently, Colt and Jack's playful rivalry went all the way back to when they were kids. But it was obvious they'd do anything for each other. Which is why Colt still worked at the diner a few hours a week when he should be focusing on his new endeavor.

"How are things going with the restaurant? Didn't your first guest check in today?"

"Yeah, but she just wanted the apple-and-walnut salad delivered to her room, so Kat said she'd take care of it. That way I could help out here."

Colt chopped a new batch of potatoes for the fryer, his features brightening the second he started talking about the restaurant. "Right now, Kat handles breakfast, which mostly consists of my mom's famous pumpkin spice cinnamon rolls. I'm in charge of lunch and dinner. We're sticking with a limited menu and a short service window at first. But in a few weeks, we'll offer the whole shebang. We want to open to the general public, too. But we'll need a few more servers and kitchen staff for that. We're trying not to get ahead of ourselves, just focusing on the current guests." He paused, his eyes glinting with excitement. "Speaking of guests, did you hear who's checking in tomorrow?"

"No. Someone interesting?"

"I'll say. None other than Landon Morris."

Vick frowned. The name didn't ring a bell, but based on Colt's tone, he guessed it was someone important. "Who?"

"Landon Morris," Colt repeated, as though saying it a second time would jog Vick's memory.

Vick stared blankly, and Colt rolled his eyes. "*The* Landon Morris, the billionaire entrepreneur from San Francisco. He was at Grant and Eliza's wedding a few months back."

"Sounds vaguely familiar." Vick shrugged, generally unimpressed.

"The guy's a brilliant chemical engineer with a passion for sustainability. He owns his own private jet *and* a helicopter. Apparently, he's also a philanthropist and isn't bad looking, either. So I've heard, anyway. Penny and some of the girls were talking about him last night, scheming over who to set him up with."

The tidbit made Vick's heart rate kick up a notch. "Who'd they have in mind?"

"The usual victims."

"Who *are*?" Vick pressed, more desperate to know than he wanted to admit.

"Anyone single under the age of eighty. Sadie, Isabella, Lucy…."

The second Colt said her name, Vick's stomach vaulted into his throat. They wanted to set up Lucy with a handsome billionaire?

Great. Just great.

He didn't know why he cared. It wasn't like he wanted dibs or anything.

"Why?" Colt narrowed his gaze, his mouth half-cocked into a smirk. "Do you have your eye on anyone I mentioned?"

"Nope." Vick added a dill pickle wedge to the El Dorado—Jack's spicy take on a tri-tip sandwich—and passed the plate to the server who breezed through the swinging door.

Vick kept his back to Colt in case his expression gave anything away, but in his peripheral vision, he caught Colt's grin widening.

And in that moment, he had a feeling he wasn't fooling anyone.

Including himself.

~

Lightly tapping her finger on the desk, Lucy stared at the laptop screen, trying to decide between two nearly identical photographs to use as a closing image for the video.

"Are you almost done?" Sadie asked from her cross-legged position on the floor.

Fitz rested his furry head in her lap, his hopeful gaze fixed on each popcorn kernel Sadie popped into her mouth.

The giant fluffy dog had become a frequent visitor ever since Lucy moved into the tiny guest house behind Jack's cabin. They particularly enjoyed watching old musicals together like *An American in Paris* and *Seven Brides for Seven Brothers*. Lucy, a skilled soprano, would sing the melody, hitting all the high notes, while Fitz howled. He could use a little work on the harmony, but he had potential.

Tonight, they'd chosen *While You Were Sleeping*, resurrecting an old tradition Lucy and Sadie started when they were in third grade. They used to watch the Sandra Bullock classic every autumn to kick off the holiday season.

"Almost finished." With a decisive click of the mouse, Lucy chose the photo on the right. Within a few minutes, she'd uploaded the completed video to YouTube, and inserted three links into the description below.

One for the Whispering Winds Inn and one for the Morning Glory Inn, since Kat wanted to share the publicity with Trudy.

Lastly, she added the website for the veterans shelter in San Francisco, hoping people would be inspired to donate.

After closing her laptop, she joined Sadie and Fitz on the pile of blankets as the opening credits rolled across the TV screen. The peppy, upbeat music filled the cozy space, muffling the howling wind outside.

"How are the videos going?" Sadie asked, offering Fitz a dog treat, which he eagerly gobbled out of her palm.

"Better than I expected," Lucy admitted. "And guess who's checking in tomorrow?"

"Who?"

"Landon Morris." Lucy watched her friend's reaction, expecting her to be impressed.

Instead, Sadie grunted, grabbing a fistful of popcorn.

"What?" She couldn't fathom why Sadie had reacted with so much hostility. They'd met Landon at Grant and Eliza's wedding, and he'd been perfectly charming—kind and generous, even if a tad bit cocky.

"Did you see his latest interview?" Sadie asked.

"No." She didn't keep tabs on celebrities. And neither did Sadie, for that matter. Curious, she asked, "Why? What did he say?"

"He said sugar is an addiction that's destroying America."

Yikes. No wonder Sadie didn't care for the guy. "Are you sure those were his exact words?" She could agree that the *over*consumption might be a problem.

"Oh, I'm sure." As if in protest, she tore open a bag of saltwater taffy she'd brought from her shop. "He also said most candy suppliers are no better than tobacco companies. Tobacco! Can you believe it?"

Lucy frowned. She couldn't remember ever seeing Sadie so upset. "Okay, that might be a little extreme."

"You think?" Sadie snorted.

"But," Lucy added, trying to calm her down, "maybe it was taken out of context. I'm sure he didn't mean small, local stores like yours. I'm sure if you talked to him and—"

"No thanks." Sadie shook her head, her straw-colored hair nearly wobbling out of her messy bun. "I have no intention of ever talking to that sugar hater."

"Now who's being extreme? You won't even *talk* to him?"

Sadie shrugged. "If you can't say something nice..."

Exasperated, Lucy sighed, switching her gaze to the TV.

She couldn't help being a little disappointed. In the back of her mind, she'd thought about setting the two of them up. Grant and Eliza always had the nicest things to say about Landon.

Plus, she'd hoped concentrating on someone else's love life would help get her thoughts off of her own—or lack thereof.

But clearly, that wasn't going to happen.

Her phone buzzed on the coffee table, and she groaned when she saw the message from her mother.

Brennan and his parents are coming over for dinner tomorrow. They specifically asked if you'll be there. I know it would mean a lot to them if you could spare a few hours.

"What is it?" Sadie asked.

"My mom's been trying to set me up with a guy I went to high school with, and she's not taking no for an answer."

She quickly texted back.

Sorry, I can't make it. Please send my apologies and warm regards.

Her mother immediately responded with a frowny-face emoji.

Followed by several more.

And a random clown emoji.

But the last one was probably a mistake.

Lucy set her phone back on the coffee table, screen down.

"What's wrong with him?"

"Nothing. He's perfectly nice. I'm just not interested."

"Why not? Is there someone else? A dark-eyed, brooding marine, perhaps?" Sadie teased.

Blushing, Lucy yanked the bag of taffy out of her hand. "No more addictive sugar for you. It's affecting your brain."

Sadie laughed, and Lucy prayed she'd only picked up on her crush because they'd been friends for so long.

She'd be mortified if anyone else figured it out.

Especially Vick.

CHAPTER 8

Vick leaned against the side of his Jeep, waiting for Lucy.

It had been a few days since he'd seen her, and he begrudged the physical ache in his chest that revealed how much he missed her.

She brought a certain quality to his day—his existence—that he found difficult to explain, but it ran deeper than enjoyment or even companionship.

He straightened, his pulse spiking when she emerged through the double doors.

Tossing him a wave, she skipped down the steps, her calf-length cardigan billowing around her long legs. As she strode toward him, her boots crunching against the gravel, the fallen leaves danced at her feet as though they relished her presence as much as he did.

What was it about this woman that captivated everything around her? Was it her glow of optimism? Her unwavering smile? Something about her aura made him believe anything was possible, which was perhaps the most dangerous quality of all.

His mother had been like that—all sunshine and roses in the midst of shadows and rubble.

And where had it gotten her?

He glanced at his forearms folded in front of his torso, catching a glimpse of the eagle tattoo. With an agitated tug, he pulled the sleeves of his sweater down to his wrists before opening the passenger door for Lucy.

"Good morning!" With a bright smile, she brushed past him and hopped inside.

"Morning." The scent of her perfume lingered in the brisk air, and he quickly shut the door.

Not that it mattered. The sultry blend of amber and vanilla filled the cab of the Jeep, distracting him as he backed out of the parking spot.

"I'm so excited for today!" Lucy gushed. "The Readathon was one of my favorite traditions growing up."

"What is it, exactly?"

"It's something Beverly started well over a decade ago to celebrate National Book Month. Basically, it's a fun excuse to read all day. There's even a contest to see who can read for the most consecutive hours without interruption."

"That explains it," Vick muttered with an incredulous shake of his head.

"Explains what?"

"Why I saw Bill Tucker reading *The Count of Monte Cristo* on the back of a riding lawnmower this morning."

"Oh, no." Lucy giggled. "Technically, the contestants have to read inside the library in order to be officially counted for the contest, but I have heard some odd stories over the years. Apparently, Mac Houston managed to stack an entire pyramid of canned soup at the front of his store while reading *Stillwatch* by Mary Higgins Clark. He didn't drop a single one"—her eyes glinted mischievously—"until the murderer was revealed, and he was so startled by the discovery, he backed into the tower and the whole thing toppled over."

Envisioning the blunder like a scene from a slapstick comedy, Vick laughed, louder than he had in a long time.

Lucy stole a glance in his direction, looking half surprised and half pleased.

Suddenly self-conscious, he cleared his throat. "What about you? Did you ever participate in the contest?"

"A few times. I never won, but I had fun, anyway." She leaned her head back, a soft, dreamy expression overtaking her countenance. "I wonder if anyone's using my special reading spot this year."

"Where is it?"

"It's a secret. If you're lucky, I might show you."

His heartbeat did a strange little two-step at the teasing tone in her voice. He tried not to read into it.

As they drove toward town, she regaled him with more humorous anecdotes of past Readathons.

For some reason, Vick loved that Lucy liked to read. Perhaps because it was one of the first—and only—things they had in common.

He found himself wanting to know all of her favorite books, which ones made her laugh and cry, which ones she threw across the room in frustration or stayed up way too late trying to finish. Which character did she most admire? Who was her secret crush?

As the last question materialized in his mind, his thoughts flew to what Colt said about Landon Morris a few days ago, and his fingers tensed on the steering wheel.

He tried to convince himself that he wasn't jealous, but who was he kidding? He hated the idea of that guy—or any guy—sweeping Lucy off of her feet.

Even as he made the internal confession, guilt knotted his stomach. He had no right to care one way or the other.

He'd finally submitted his job application as a deckhand on the *Lucky Lure*, and received a response less than twenty-four hours later. They'd be departing out of the Dutch Harbor November 1, on the hunt for king crab.

He told himself the arrangement couldn't be more perfect. He'd work on and off aboard various fishing boats throughout the year, and the rest of the time he'd hunker down in a remote cabin, keeping to himself. He could read, enjoy nature, and revel in peaceful solitude.

Which is exactly what he wanted out of life... wasn't it?

~

As they climbed the broad stone steps of the historic library, Lucy's heart fluttered in anticipation.

She'd always adored the old brick building with its stately alabaster columns and tall, elegant windows with matching white trim.

On the wooden bench flanking the front door, two teens huddled over the final book in *The Lord of the Rings* trilogy, their enraptured gazes glued to the page. In fact, all around town, the air hummed with the current of countless imaginations engrossed in fanciful, fictional worlds.

Time seemed suspended as couples lounged on picnic blankets beneath the shady oak tree in the town square. A woman strolled down Main Street, reading while she walked, barely sidestepping a lamppost at the last minute.

It wasn't until Vick cleared his throat that she realized she'd been standing with her hand on the brass doorknob, taking in the bibliophile's paradise before them.

Ducking inside, she inhaled deeply as the scent of aged paper and pungent ink flooded her senses, transporting her back to her childhood.

Even though no one spoke, there was an almost audible

quality to the energy permeating the room. Adults and children alike were tucked into every nook and cranny, devouring classics and contemporary novels with unabashed fervor.

"Welcome," Beverly greeted them with a warm, velvety whisper. "If you're here for the competition, I'm afraid you're a bit late. We started at seven this morning."

"Actually," Lucy said softly, "we're here to take a few photos and some video footage, if that's all right."

Beverly nodded, but pressed a finger to her lips, suggesting they work quietly.

Lucy placed a hand over her heart, silently promising they'd be as unobtrusive as possible.

It wasn't easy to get the footage she needed without speaking, but Vick picked up on her nonverbal cues remarkably well. And she reasoned she could add a voice-over narration later.

When they'd taken enough photos in the main room, Lucy gestured for Vick to follow her toward the back of the library. As they neared her old haunt, her pulse beat like the persistent tapping of a typewriter.

She eased open a creaking door and slipped inside, tugging Vick behind her. "Here we are," she announced, her voice dripping with reverence.

"A supply closet?" His gaze swept the cluttered, dusty shelves and collection of cleaning supplies.

"You have to look closer." She stepped around a tall filing cabinet and caught her breath.

A round bow window jutted out from the back wall, capturing an idyllic view of the garden behind the library. The smooth wooden seat offered just enough space for a young girl to recline with a book.

A book...

Struck by a fleeting memory, she rushed toward the window and ran her finger along the lip of the seat. Feeling the groove, she lifted the solid panel of wood, revealing a hidden storage space underneath.

"What are you doing?" Vick asked.

Too enthralled to speak, she didn't answer. Her heart thrumming with excitement, she reached into the compartment and gingerly removed a well-loved copy of *Peter Pan and Wendy*.

"Is that—" Vick stepped toward her, then paused, his eyes wide and questioning.

"Before you tattle on me to Beverly, this is my book, not the library's." She cracked open the worn spine, cradling the buttery binding carefully as a few loose pages nearly slipped onto the floor.

The hand-painted illustrations were just as beautiful as she remembered—maybe more so.

All those years ago, she'd brought it to the library to read, and had completely forgotten which of her many hiding places she'd used to protect it from the grubby hands of her brothers. She'd been devastated when they moved to Primrose Valley and she couldn't find it.

She glanced up and met Vick's gaze, puzzled by his strained features.

While she couldn't quite read his expression, she immediately sensed something was off.

CHAPTER 9

Vick couldn't believe it. Out of all the books in the world, *this* was her favorite?

"Is something wrong?" Her voice laced with concern, Lucy held the threadbare binding to her chest, completely unaware of its significance.

At least, the significance to him... and his mother.

He swallowed, wincing against the sensation of coarse sand sifting down his throat.

Even after all these years, he could picture her clearly in his mind, like a movie frozen on the screen. When he was young, she must have read the book to him a thousand times or more. He knew most of it by heart—each whimsical allegory and poignant truth wrapped in unapologetic playfulness.

Since her death, he'd blocked every single word from his memory, afraid of what they might tell him.

"No, nothing's wrong," he said with a casual inflection that almost convinced himself. "I was just surprised, that's all."

"By my hiding spot?" she asked, some of the tension slipping from her tone.

"I definitely wasn't expecting it."

A soft smile smoothed her worry lines, and she explained, "Growing up, I didn't have many books to call my own, and the ones I did have, my brothers liked to steal. They'd drop them in puddles or get grimy fingerprints all over them. I had to hide them to keep them safe." Wistfully, she ran her hand over the timeworn cover. "This one was my favorite. Have you read it?"

"A long time ago." Haunting memories wrapped around his chest like a strangle knot, cinching tighter as he struggled against them.

He tried to remain calm as the walls of the confined storage space crept closer together, forcing the oxygen out of the room.

Lucy eased open the book again, turning the pages with a tender touch. "There are so many brilliant lines in this novel. Like this one: 'When the first baby laughed for the first time, its laugh broke into a thousand pieces, and they all went skipping about, and that was the beginning of fairies.'"

As though reliving the tale quote by quote, she shared a few more of her favorites.

Each time she spoke, Vick's heartbeat pounded louder against his eardrums, reaching a near-deafening volume.

His hands shaking, he drew the tip of each finger to his thumb, one after the other, inhaling and exhaling in long, labored breaths.

He wanted her to stop, but she couldn't hear his silent plea, too engrossed in her nostalgic return to Neverland.

"Oh, this passage about Mrs. Darling is one of the most beautiful and enchanting paragraphs ever written." Her features brightened, and she read in a dreamy voice, "'She was a lovely lady, with a romantic mind and such a sweet mocking mouth. Her romantic mind was like the tiny boxes, one within the other, that come from the puzzling East, however many you discover there is always one more; and her sweet mocking mouth had one kiss on it that Wendy could never get, though there it was, perfectly conspicuous in the right-hand corner.'"

Beaming, she looked up, as though expecting him to share in her delight.

The mirth in her eyes instantly faded, and he could see his sadness reflected in the deep pools of blue. "Vick, what's wrong? Was it something I said?" Her pitch rose, the worry lines reappearing across her brow.

He swallowed again, but this time, the grains of sand had turned to glass. "It was my mom's favorite book, too."

"*Was*?" she asked softly, barely above a whisper.

"She passed away several years ago." His voice sounded like it belonged to someone else. And, in a way, he almost wished that it did.

That would mean it was someone else's mother—and someone else's pain.

"I'm so sorry." She snapped the book shut. "I shouldn't have gone on and on about it."

Her concern and compassionate self-reproof generated a welcoming calmness, grounding him back in the present and lowering his guard. "My mom would've liked you. She always said you could tell a lot about a person by the books they read."

His own admission surprised him, and a shy blush stole across her cheeks, but neither of them broke their gaze.

The air between them sizzled with a connection he couldn't explain—something soft and fragile like a thread, yet as volatile as a live wire.

Her lips parted, but hesitation sparked in her eyes.

He shifted his weight, leaning forward a fraction of an inch, desperate to know what she was about to say.

~

Lucy paused, paralyzed by uncertainty.

She didn't want this moment to end. The tether

between them had never felt so strong, but she knew it could snap in a single second if she wasn't careful.

A million questions circled in her mind. She wanted to know anything and everything about Vick's mother, his childhood, what had been most transformative in his life.

But she could sense his walls lifting. If she wanted to know more, she would need to tread lightly.

She'd need to be vulnerable herself—a terrifying prospect.

Gathering a breath, she blurted, "Would you like to have lunch with me? We could talk more about our favorite books."

As soon as she said the words, she wanted to take them back.

What if he said no?

Her fears tumbled, collecting more doubts the longer he took to respond.

After a few agonizing seconds, he said, "Sure."

One word. One syllable.

But to Lucy, it carried the weight of the entire world.

She struggled to keep her beating heart from pounding right out of her chest. "Great," she said coolly. "The bistro?"

"Sure."

There was that word again.

That beautiful, underrated word.

If written on a page, it would've been blazed in gold.

As they headed back to the main part of the library, Lucy mulled over every topic she wanted to touch on, and how she would bring them up. Or maybe she should simply sit back and let Vick guide the conversation? After all, wasn't the best part about sharing a meal with someone the natural pockets of opportunity to simply listen?

Good grief. She'd never been more nervous in all her life.

They'd almost reached the front door when Beverly stopped her with a gentle hand on her arm. "Did you get everything you needed, dear?"

"Yes, thank you." Lucy smiled, mentally adding, And far more than I'd expected.

"I hate to ask..." Beverly wrung her hands together, her voice hesitant.

"What do you need?" Lucy prompted kindly.

"I'm worried about Frank," Beverly admitted softly, telltale creases etched into her forehead. "He's been under so much stress lately he hasn't been eating unless I remind him. I normally bring him lunch, but I'll be here all day monitoring the contest."

"I'd be happy to bring him something," Lucy assured her, ignoring the tiny pang of disappointment. "What does he like?"

"A bowl of soup from the bistro would be perfect." Gratitude relaxed Beverly's features. "I'll get my wallet."

"Don't worry about it. It'll be my treat."

"Oh, that's not necessary—"

"I know," Lucy interjected warmly. "It's my way of saying thank you for organizing this event. It's always been one of my favorites."

Beverly seemed pleased by this and relented with another grateful smile. "Well, thank you, dear. That's very kind of you."

When they stepped outside, the clouds had shifted from earlier that morning, revealing a sliver of sunlight. And although their plans had changed, she clung to the tiny ray of optimism. "It isn't exactly what I had in mind, but how would you feel about getting our lunches to-go and eating with Frank?"

She figured Beverly would appreciate the assurance that Frank had actually eaten the food they brought.

"Works for me."

Lucy tried to read his expression. Was he disappointed about it not being just the two of them? She couldn't tell one way or the other.

"To be honest," he said with a confidential inflection, "I've always been curious to know more about Frank Barrie. He seems like quite the character."

Lucy grinned at his understatement. The man's cantankerous temperament had become the stuff of legends during her childhood, almost as infamous as Captain Hook himself.

Although he'd changed a lot in the last few years, she was suddenly curious to see how the unusual afternoon would unfold.

And what new connections, if any, it would provide for her and Vick.

CHAPTER 10

Vick didn't mention it to Lucy, but he'd always sensed a certain kinship with Frank Barrie. He'd heard Frank served in the navy, and Vick understood the older man's impulse to isolate himself from the rest of the town.

But what fascinated Vick the most—whether he'd admit it out loud or not—was Frank's ability to overcome this part of himself, to reenter society as a committed member of the community despite the decades of self-inflicted solitude.

He wanted to know *why*… for reasons he couldn't quite articulate. Or perhaps, more accurately, that he didn't want to face.

Lucy directed him to turn down the next street, and the road transitioned from badly paved asphalt to neatly kept dirt and gravel.

Towering sycamores arched overhead, their autumn leaves an array of mottled browns and yellow. Around the bend, a moss-green farmhouse came into view. Vick immediately noticed the rocking chairs on the front porch and the bench swing with cozy pillows, slightly swaying in the pleasant breeze.

He thought of the single rocking chair at his place and couldn't help making a mental comparison.

Before exiting the Jeep, he reached for the take-out bag from the bistro, but Lucy had already grabbed it and slid from the passenger seat.

He joined her in the driveway and followed her wide-eyed gaze toward the smoke rising above the pitched roof.

The distinct, heady aroma of roasting coffee mingled with the damp, earthy scent of impending rain, and Vick filled his lungs with the invigorating combination.

"I didn't think he was supposed to roast on his own," Lucy murmured with a cautious edge, before admitting, "but I've always wanted to watch."

"Then we shouldn't let the opportunity pass us by." He motioned for her to follow him around the side of the house, his own curiosity propelling each footstep.

A few years ago, he'd picked up seasonal work in an almond-packing facility and learned how they were roasted, but nothing prepared him for what they saw when they rounded the corner.

Frank Barrie stood beside a tall metal contraption, similar in size and shape to an almond roaster, which used hot air to tumble the nuts inside a cavernous chamber, ensuring even heat distribution.

But that's where the similarities ended.

With a swift motion, Frank yanked a lever on the machine and a barrage of crackling beans poured into a large metal cylinder. Aromatic vapor escaped through tiny perforations punched on all sides.

Vick realized he'd been holding his breath, waiting to see what would happen next. He exhaled sharply when Frank glanced up, meeting his gaze.

He'd encountered many intimidating men during his time in the Marines, but Frank's icy gray stare topped them all.

He braced himself for a harsh reprimand, but to his surprise, Frank waved him over.

Vick cast an uncertain glance at Lucy, but she merely gawked and gave a small, helpless shrug.

"I don't have all day, son," Frank bellowed above the loud rumble of the machine.

The authoritative boom of Frank's voice reminded Vick of his time in boot camp, and his instincts kicked in.

Rushing over, he dutifully obeyed as Frank barked instructions, walking him through the remaining steps of the roasting process.

Through it all, Vick didn't have time to be nervous or second-guess himself. Fueled by intrigue and adrenaline, he followed Frank's orders with militant precision, relishing the exhilaration of the experience.

While he hadn't expected coffee roasting to require so much strength and stamina, he appreciated the physicality of the movements and the challenge of utilizing different muscles in his body.

It was no wonder Frank's doctors had asked him to cut back, despite being in excellent shape for a man in his eighties.

Vick couldn't help wondering what Frank thought he was doing, starting a roast on his own. But he didn't have long to dwell on the question.

The final stage of the process consisted of letting the hot beans sweat out their excess moisture in five-gallon mason jars.

"Let it sit for a few minutes," Frank said gruffly. "Then dump the beans back into the basin, wipe down the condensation in the jars with this towel, then refill them. Got it?"

"Yes, sir." Vick stopped a second short of saluting.

"Good. When you're done, you may join this young lady and myself inside." Frank gifted Lucy with something close to a smile. "I take it Bevy sent you over here to check on me?"

"We come bearing lunch." Lucy lifted the bag containing butternut squash soup and the Buttercup Bistro's famous Mother Lode Stew.

Vick noticed how she'd deftly sidestepped the babysitting allegation, although it carried more than a hint of truth.

"Then let's eat, so you can give a glowing report to the warden." He shot Lucy a wink, and she grinned.

Vick watched them disappear up the back steps into the house, realizing he didn't mind being left behind to finish up.

He'd enjoyed himself more than he'd expected, and he took a moment to revel in the sensation of excess adrenaline seeping from his extremities.

It had been a long time since he'd felt that kind of rush.

Unless he counted every second spent with Lucy.

~

Growing up, Lucy had been terrified of the grumpy old man who lived in the woods. When she was really young, a few of her brothers had told her scary stories about how he liked to eat little girls for breakfast and dipped their fingers and toes in his morning coffee as though dunking almond biscotti.

As an adult, she felt terrible about the unkind rumors. Especially since Frank had turned out to be a lovely man whose heartache and pain had driven him to a life of bitterness and isolation. It had taken a caring, persistent person like Cassie to wear down his walls.

Now, looking around his kitchen, she never would've guessed his gloomy past. Sunlight streamed through lace-trimmed curtains, lending a soft glow to the homey space. Beverly had adorned the pleasant pale-blue walls with decorative china plates and framed literary quotes.

But Frank had his own presence in the plethora of coffee paraphernalia. Both hand and electric bean grinders, a French press, pour over, compact espresso machine, and a few other devices she didn't recognize. His best-selling book, *The Mariposa*

Method, and the second edition he'd cowritten with Cassie, claimed a prominent position on the counter between a ceramic cookie jar and a brass-plated coffeepot.

"Do your knees bend?" Frank quipped.

Lucy realized she'd been standing and staring for several minutes while he scooped ground coffee into the bottom of a French press.

With a sheepish grin, she sank onto one of the chairs at the small, antique dining table and unpacked the brown paper bag from the bistro—stew for the guys and butternut squash for herself. They'd also included several slices of still-warm sourdough bread seasoned with sage and rosemary. Even from inside the tightly closed containers, the mouthwatering aroma filled the room, mingling with the scent of freshly ground coffee.

Luckily, the squeal of the teakettle muffled the loud growl of her stomach.

After pouring boiling water over the grounds, Frank situated the lid of the French press and let it sit. Turning toward her, he narrowed his thick, peppery eyebrows, pinning her with his steely gaze. "There's a candied maple pecan pie in the bread box. Should we eat it now or after lunch?"

Lucy hesitated, sensing a trap. Which answer was the right one? She decided to answer honestly. "I've always been a dessert-first kind of gal, myself."

"I had a feeling."

She released the breath she'd been holding, smiling when she caught the twinkle in his eyes.

"Plates are in there." He nodded toward the cupboard.

As she set the table, Frank sliced generous servings of rich, gooey pie.

Right on time, the back door creaked open.

Vick entered the room, exuding a palpable air of satisfaction.

Not to mention a grin that made her heart stop beating.

She'd never seen him like this, so happy and content. It was a good look on him. One she wanted to see a lot more often.

"Did you burn the place down?" Frank asked.

"No, sir. It went smoothly." His gaze landed on the book wedged between the cookie jar and coffeepot. "May I?"

Frank tilted his head in what appeared to be a nod, and Vick slid the thick, glossy hardback from its resting place.

He thumbed through the pages, Frank watching him out of the corner of his eye as he poured three cups of dark, velvety coffee.

From her perch at the table, Lucy observed the exchange, noting how Frank appeared to be studying Vick, as though appraising him.

"Army?" Frank asked, seemingly out of nowhere.

"Marines, sir."

"And now you work at the diner?"

"Yes, sir."

"But not for long?" Frank's question sounded more like a statement.

Vick slowly closed the book, some of the color leaving his face.

Was it her imagination or was he exerting extra effort to avoid looking in her direction?

"Yes, sir," he said after a lengthy pause.

"And are you running toward or away from something?"

Frank didn't seem concerned with his blunt line of questioning, and Lucy marveled at his boldness. She also silently applauded him. From the moment Kat mentioned Vick would be leaving soon, she longed to know why, no matter how badly it stung.

Leaning forward, she anxiously awaited Vick's response.

"I'm… not sure how to answer that."

"I suspected as much," Frank said, though not unkindly. "May I suggest you figure it out sooner rather than later?"

"Yes, sir."

Frank gestured for Vick to take a seat at the table, and Vick moved to slide the book back into place.

"Keep it," Frank told him, handing Lucy a mug with aromatic steam wafting from the rim.

"I couldn't do that, sir."

"You'd be doing me a favor. I have copies coming out of my ears, which makes it awfully hard to trim the stray hairs in the morning."

Frank shot Lucy another wink and caught her so off guard with his unexpected humor, she nearly choked on her first sip of coffee.

Even Vick cracked a small grin. "Okay, then. I will. Thank you." He joined them at the table.

The conversation switched to lighter subjects, but Lucy noticed Vick still avoided her gaze, almost going out of his way not to address her directly.

Did it have anything to do with the topic of him leaving soon? And if so, did his discomfort imply some sort of deeper connection, perhaps even regret?

If only she could be as bold as Frank and simply ask Vick outright.

Did their time together mean anything at all?

Or was it simply wishful thinking?

CHAPTER 11

On the drive back to the inn, Vick waited for Lucy to mention his plans to leave town. When she didn't, he couldn't decide if he felt relief or disappointment.

On the one hand, he wasn't sure what he'd say if the topic came up. On the other, a not-so-small part of him wanted to believe he'd be missed.

Which, he realized, wasn't fair.

What had started as a faint drizzle when they left Frank's increased to heavy downpour, hammering the windshield, and he flicked on the wipers. The gentle *swish* harmonized with the howling wind and steady rhythm of raindrops, working together to drown out the conspicuous silence.

When had his life become so complicated? He used to enjoy traveling the country, packing up his belongings every few years to explore uncharted territory. Thoughts of settling down hadn't crept into his mind until moving to Poppy Creek—until meeting Lucy.

He stole a sideways glance in her direction. She leaned against the headrest, gazing out the rain-spattered window to the misty landscape beyond. *Peter Pan and Wendy* lay in her lap, partially covered by her palms. She looked deep in thought, her thumb gently grazing the soft leather binding.

For a fleeting moment, a strange, almost overpowering urge to reach across the console and hold her hand overcame him. He gave a sharp shake of his head, dismissing the ridiculous impulse, and forced his attention back on the road.

Swish, swish, swish.

Vick wished the wipers could clear away his troubled thoughts. They kept wandering to passages from the book—passages he'd worked hard to forget.

He could still see the way Lucy's face lit up, illuminated with joy and fondness as she recited the section about Mrs. Darling and her elusive kiss. The meaning behind it had been long-debated among literary scholars, but Vick had his own theory.

He stole another glimpse of Lucy.

Even now, lost in her own rumination, the corner of her mouth tipped up—a hint of her ever-present smile. He used to attribute it to her easy, carefree lifestyle. A byproduct of never knowing deep, soul-searing pain.

But what if his assumptions were wrong? Would he be better off not knowing?

It seemed the more he learned about her, the more entangled his heart became.

He pulled up to the inn, parking beside her Mercedes. Even though they'd spent all afternoon together, he found himself grasping for reasons to delay their goodbye. "What are your plans for the rest of the day?"

He suddenly remembered Landon Morris had checked in recently and wondered if they'd crossed paths yet.

"After I compile today's video, I thought I'd get some reading in before the day's end." She tucked the book beneath her sweater to shield it from the downpour. "What about you?"

"Same." He nodded toward Frank's book on the dash.

For a moment, he debated suggesting they read somewhere

together, envisioning a cozy blanket, mugs of hot chocolate, and companionable silence save for the soothing refrain of the storm.

But he hesitated too long, and she reached for the door handle.

Vick made a move to hop out and open it for her, but she waved aside his gesture. "I've got it." With a forceful jiggle, she shoved it open and slid out into the pelting rain.

Quickly, she ducked inside her car, and within minutes, she'd vanished in the haze.

As he watched her drive away, Frank's question materialized in his mind.

Are you running toward or away from something?

He really wished he knew.

~

When she got home, Lucy switched on her electric teakettle and sat at her laptop to load the footage from the library.

Images of herself popped onto the screen, and she peered closer, her stomach swirling as she studied them.

Ever since she started this project with Vick, she'd noticed an unusual phenomenon. He had an uncanny knack of capturing her most nuanced expressions and mannerisms. The moment during her laugh when the bridge of her nose crinkled. Her self-conscious tick of tucking a strand of hair behind her left ear, just so. He seemed to catch an intimacy between her and the camera, as if there were times her gaze penetrated the lens.

Which made her feel both vulnerable and deeply seen.

It had to mean *something*, didn't it?

She'd formed a habit of asking herself that very question multiple times a day, as if persistence could make an answer appear.

But no matter how desperately she wanted things to be different, the fact remained: Vick would be leaving soon.

And he still hadn't talked to her about it.

She'd waited for him to bring it up on the drive back to the inn, but he'd hardly said a word.

Was it time she gave up hoping for something more?

The kettle clicked off, and she rose to fix herself a cup of cinnamon chai.

She stood at the kitchenette window, watching raindrops scatter across the ethereal surface of the lake, the regal mountains in the distance hidden behind a veil of mist.

In moments like this one—faced with the incomparable beauty and solace—she couldn't imagine living anywhere else. And these moments were becoming increasingly more frequent.

But whenever she pictured her life in Poppy Creek, pieces of the puzzle were missing, creating a jumbled, incomplete image.

She thought of Frank's question for Vick, whether he was running toward or away from something.

In her case, it was definitely toward.

But toward *what*, she wasn't sure.

Once her tea had steeped, she returned to her makeshift desk at the small, two-person table by the window and spent the next few hours compiling all of the photos and video footage, adding music and a voice-over. On a whim, she also included an additional link for a nonprofit children's literacy program.

The internet connection was slower than normal due to the storm, so she scrolled through comments on previous videos while the new one loaded.

Her heart warmed at all the sweet and enthusiastic comments gushing over Poppy Creek and the town's unusual celebrations. People really seemed to respond to the strong sense of community. And dozens of viewers said they couldn't wait to visit.

Of course, there were other comments, too. The ones she instantly deleted. Usually men who made inappropriate and crude comments on her appearance. And a few trolls who competed against each other to be the most offensive person on the internet.

There were times she wanted to delete her account altogether, to save herself from the toxic vitriol. But then she thought about all the kindness she'd experienced and the countless positive interactions.

Especially now, witnessing firsthand how engagement online could lead to tangible benefits for Jack and Kat, not to mention the various charities and organizations she'd promoted. She hadn't expected the videos to make such an impact. And if they made a difference, even in a small way, she could endure a bit of negative feedback, couldn't she?

She rose to refill her mug, swaying as she stood. Placing a palm on the table, she steadied herself, figuring she must have gotten up too quickly.

After waiting a moment for the dizzy spell to pass, she shuffled into the kitchen.

As she lifted the kettle and poured the steaming liquid into her cup, black spots blurred her vision.

She wobbled slightly, splashing droplets of hot water on her hand.

With a pained yelp, she yanked her hand away and the kettle clattered against the countertop. She pressed her cool lips to the wound, stumbling backward as the floor beneath her seemed to lurch sideways.

Wobbly and disoriented, she staggered toward the couch, collapsing onto the cushions.

Even lying down, the room continued to spin like the ride at the county fair that had made her regret eating all that funnel cake.

She squeezed her eyes shut, draping an arm across her face to block out the offending light.

The pressure against her temples increased like a clamp tightening, but the pain wasn't nearly as debilitating as last time. She wasn't sure whether to be relieved or worried.

A part of her wished for some sense of predictability. Maybe then she could manage her life around each episode.

Instead, they tormented her with their irregularity—both timing and symptoms. How could she live with that kind of uncertainty?

Each time another migraine assailed her, she promised herself she'd make an appointment with the specialist.

But as soon as it faded, and her world slowly returned to normal, she'd change her mind, telling herself the same lie. *That was the last one. Things will be okay now.*

But what if they weren't?

So far, she'd been alone and somewhere safe whenever they struck.

But what if she wasn't so lucky next time?

CHAPTER 12

Vick sat at the bar, oblivious to the noisy diner around him. He propped his chin on both hands, forcing his eyes open as he watched Rhett plop two scoops of bourbon vanilla ice cream into a frosty old-fashioned soda glass.

Next came the drizzle of homemade chocolate sauce that required a special swirling technique, but Vick wasn't paying attention.

His heavy eyelids drifted shut.

He'd stayed awake all night finishing Frank's book, and he was paying the price this afternoon.

Or rather, *Rhett* was paying the price.

Vick was supposed to be teaching him how to make their famous sarsaparilla floats, but he kept dozing off.

The pop of the soda bottle lid jolted him awake, and he nearly fell off the stool.

Rhett chuckled. "Didn't get much sleep last night?"

"More like *no* sleep," Vick mumbled, reaching for a chilled sarsaparilla. Maybe the cold and carbonation would help.

Rhett flashed a knowing smile as he poured the velvety brown liquid over the mounds of ice cream, tilting the glass to combat the foam. "Does it have anything to do with that girl I've seen you with around town?"

Vick sputtered, choking on the soda in his surprise. He pounded his fist against his chest a few times, waiting for the bubbles to settle. "Uh, no. I got sucked into a book."

"Ah." Rhett nodded. "That's happened to me more than once." He topped the float with whipped cream before adding, "But that girl, you two are together, right?"

"Me and Lucy?" Vick asked, buying time. He knew exactly who Rhett meant.

"The tall blond with the nice smile."

Vick gulped the licorice-flavored beverage, ignoring the way the fizz burned the back of his throat as he rummaged through his mind for a response.

His gut—and every fiber in his being, if he were honest—wanted to proclaim to the world that they were most definitely an item.

But despite his moments of delusion, he knew it couldn't be further from the truth.

"We're not *together* together. I'm helping her with a promotional project for the inn."

"That's too bad." Rhett topped the whipped cream with chocolate shavings and a maraschino cherry and slid the float toward him. "You two make a good-looking couple."

Vick didn't disagree. Although, in his opinion, Lucy carried most of the weight in the looks department. Not that he was a slouch or anything.

For some reason, he liked that Rhett assumed they were dating. Maybe that meant the connection he felt between them wasn't just inside his own head.

Not that it mattered either way. Even if he wasn't leaving soon, Lucy was way out of his league.

He worked in a diner and lived in an oversize soup can while

Lucy could have anything she wanted in life.

Plus, Lucy's parents were Primrose Valley royalty and his...

He winced at the pang of guilt that rippled through him.

Where had that thought come from? He'd always been proud of his mom. They may not have had much to call their own, but nobody worked harder or loved more deeply.

Now, his father was a different story. His mother met him in an acting class and they married impulsively four months later, then got pregnant shortly thereafter. The louse abandoned her in her third trimester and never looked back.

No alimony. No child support. No cards on his birthday. He never came by to see him, not even once.

When his mother died, he thought about looking for him. But what would've been the point?

Moving the focus off of himself, Vick took a sip from the extra-large straw and asked, "So, Rhett, what about you? Are you seeing anyone?"

With a damp cloth, Rhett wiped a nonexistent glob of ice cream off the counter. "I haven't dated since my divorce."

"Oh, man. I'm sorry. Divorce is tough. Do you have kids?"

"One, but we're not close."

"Sorry to hear that. Maybe that'll change one day," Vick offered hopefully.

Rhett continued to scrub the sparkling countertop. "Maybe. To tell you the truth, I messed up pretty badly when I was younger, and my ex didn't want me around. She said I'd be a terrible role model, and she was right."

Vick's heart went out to the guy. Whatever his past, he'd cleaned up his act now. "Well, the holidays are coming up. It's the season of second chances."

For the first time since the conversation started, Rhett met his gaze, and a soft, tentative smile broke through his somber expression. "You may be right. Thanks."

"Speaking of second chances..." Vick flashed a rueful smile.

"The ice-cream-to-soda ratio is a little off. Try making another one, but with slightly bigger scoops this time."

"Sure thing." Rhett grabbed another glass from the mini fridge below the bar. "So, this book," he said casually, switching to a less personal topic. "I gather it was pretty good."

"I enjoyed it," Vick admitted, although it was an understatement. He'd found it riveting. He never would've guessed he'd be so fascinated by coffee roasting, but there was something about the way Frank described it. His words gripped him and wouldn't let go.

The clatter of breaking glass tore him from his thoughts.

His face ghostly pale, Rhett stared at the glittering shards scattered across the counter as though he had no idea how they got there.

"Don't worry about it," Vick told him, surprised by how rattled he looked.

The man's panicked gaze darted toward the entrance, and he took a step backward.

"I-I'll be right back." Without cleaning up the mess, Rhett retreated through the swinging door into the kitchen.

Puzzled, Vick glanced over his shoulder.

Jack greeted a petite, pleasant-looking brunette in her late forties or early fifties. Her gaze swept the diner as she followed Jack to a booth by the window.

Vick noticed her clock the emergency exits, which reminded him of his military training.

Strange.

But she hardly seemed like a threat.

So, why had Rhett bolted?

~

Lucy tried to keep a straight face while Sadie glared at her from across the table.

"Why are we eating here?" her friend hissed.

"Because the food is delicious. And I thought it would be nice to support the inn since the restaurant hasn't been open very long."

Technically, it still wasn't open to the public, but Lucy had a free pass as the owner's sister.

She stifled a laugh as Sadie glanced over her shoulder, glaring at Landon Morris while he ate a garden salad a few tables over, innocently minding his own business.

Lucy secretly hoped that putting them in such close proximity might spark a mutual interest, but no such luck so far.

Although, she was pretty sure Landon had stolen a few glances in her friend's direction.

While not classically beautiful, with her prominent bone structure and strong, athletic build, Sadie had a striking quality about her. Lucy suspected it had something to do with her unapologetic confidence and commanding stature. Either way, she was a difficult woman *not* to notice.

"Welcome, ladies." Colt approached their table with his trademark grin. "What can I get for you today?"

Sadie snapped her menu shut and said decisively, "I'll take the peach cobbler, please. À la mode." She added extra emphasis to the last bit, speaking louder than necessary.

Lucy suspected she knew for whose benefit.

"For lunch?" Colt asked, sounding surprised.

"Yes," Sadie said coolly. "And I'll have a caramel latte, as well."

Lucy buried her face in her menu, muffling her snicker. Sadie would probably put herself in a sugar coma just to prove a point. Collecting her composure, she glanced up and said, "I'll have the butternut squash ravioli. Thanks." She handed Colt their menus.

"Okay, one ravioli and a peach cobbler coming up."

When he'd returned to the kitchen, Lucy raised an eyebrow at her friend. "Really?"

"What?" Sadie shrugged. "It's not like you haven't had dessert first before."

She had a point there. In fact, she'd done it just the other day.

"What event are you and Vick covering next?" Sadie asked, taking a sip of her ice water.

"Pumpkin & Paws." Her voice bubbled with excitement. The event was held at Bill Tucker's farm every year, and in addition to a pumpkin patch and petting zoo, the animal shelter in Primrose Valley brought puppies for adoption.

"I'll be there serving my spiced apple cider alongside Maggie's pumpkin spice cinnamon rolls to raise money for the shelter." Sadie smirked as she added, "We're calling it Calories for a Cause."

"How apropos." Lucy laughed.

Just then, Kat strolled in with a new guest.

The woman wore her platinum blond hair in a sleek bob and teetered on five-inch heels. Christian Louboutin heels, to be exact. She'd recognize the red soles anywhere.

"We're open for lunch and dinner," Kat explained warmly. "And room service is available at your request."

"Fabulous. I'll be working in my room most of the week." She lifted her Dior sunglasses when she spotted Landon. "My, my. Is that who I think it is?" Without waiting for an answer, she sauntered across the room and held out her hand. "I'm Morgan Withers. It's a pleasure to finally meet you."

She said *finally* as if it were only a matter of time until important people like them crossed paths.

Only, Lucy had never heard of her before. And she didn't look familiar.

Landon stared at the woman's hand a moment, then back at

his lunch. As though with great effort, he set down his fork and shook her hand. "Landon Morris. But it appears you already know who I am."

Her shrill laugh pinged against the walls. You'd think the guy had just told the world's most hilarious joke. "May I?" She gestured to the empty seat, sitting down before he had time to respond. Directing her remark to Kat without actually looking at her, Morgan said, "I'll take a chilled LaCroix and a menu."

Kat met Lucy's gaze and gave a helpless shrug before spinning on her heel and heading for the kitchen.

"Isn't she delightful," Sadie mumbled under her breath. "They're a perfect match."

By the uncomfortable way Landon shifted in his seat, Lucy wasn't sure he agreed.

"I believe you know my client Trent Luxe." Morgan said his name with exaggerated fanfare. "He was on the hit reality show *Blind Date a Billionaire*. If I remember correctly, you were asked to be on it, too, right?"

Lucy smothered a laugh as Sadie gave a dramatic eye roll. But they were both surprised when Landon responded, "I was. But I declined," barely hiding his disdain.

"Trent is moving on, as well," Morgan quipped. "To bigger and better things. I can't say much, but we're working on a brand-new project. We're still ironing out some of the details, but I can already tell it's going to be the most talked about show on television."

"Congratulations," Landon said stiffly, clearly not impressed, which only made Lucy like him more.

The haughty woman cast an impatient glance over her shoulder, as if to see what was taking Kat so long, and her gaze locked on Lucy.

Recognition flickered in her heavily made-up eyes, and she gave her an appraising once-over.

A slow, satisfied smile spread across her blood-red lips, and something in her almost predatory expression made Lucy squirm.

Why did she suddenly feel like a helpless mouse trapped in a corner?

CHAPTER 13

From his vantage point on top of two stacked hay bales, Vick surveyed the crowd, hoping to catch sight of Rhett. Apart from working his shift at the diner, the man had made himself scarce lately.

Vick suspected it had something to do with whatever spooked him the other day, but he'd been evasive whenever Vick brought it up.

Jumping down to join the festivities, he scanned the sea of faces again, quickly discerning between the new and familiar among the kaleidoscope of colors and merriment.

Bill Tucker prided himself on hosting the Pumpkin & Paws event every year, and he'd spared no expense sprucing up the farm. Even Peggy Sue had a brand-new collar—pink plaid with a plastic sunflower stuck on the side.

If the level of mirth and gaiety was any indication, Bill's attention to detail had paid off. Happy families toured the pumpkin patch, while others brought their children to the petting zoo, mostly to see the spitting alpacas. The sound of youthful giggles and squeals carried above the clamor of rowdy lawn games like pumpkin bowling and gourd ring toss.

Several people had entered the pumpkin-carving contest and later in the day, they'd host the pumpkin parachute competition, which Vick couldn't wait to watch.

He hoped Lucy would make it in time. She was supposed to arrive twenty minutes ago, but he hadn't seen her yet.

Both she and Rhett were MIA.

Vick circled back to the dog adoption booth. The volunteers from the shelter had chosen a shady patch of lawn beneath a golden-leaved walnut tree to set up the pen for the dozens of puppies they'd brought to the event.

The last time he'd walked by, a family of five was adopting a beagle mix with the floppiest ears he'd ever seen. The five-year-old son, who also happened to have large ears, cradled the puppy in his arms, his face a picture of pure joy.

As Vick approached, his heart stuttered to a stop.

Lucy sat cross-legged in the center of the corral, covered in a wiggly pack of fur balls. Some licked her face, others chewed on her hair, a few were nuzzled in her arms and lap.

She'd thrown her head back, her blissful laughter mingling with excited barks, yips, and yaps.

The adorable vignette was too perfect to pass up.

Spotting her camera by her purse on a nearby hay bale, Vick looped the strap over his neck and unscrewed the lens cap.

He snapped a few wide-angle shots, then zoomed in on her expression, capturing the sparkle in her eyes as her laughter brought her close to tears.

One squishy butterball climbed up her shoulder and pressed its pudgy snout against her cheek, both paws splayed to the side as though hugging her face.

The two seemed made for each other, and the endearing sight stirred a warm, tingling feeling in his stomach—which he tried his best to ignore.

Lucy propped up its plump backside with her hand and snuggled the pup with her nose, cooing softly.

The tingling sensation traveled from his stomach into his chest, and Vick lowered the camera, quickly replacing the lens cap.

His face suddenly felt hot, even though it couldn't have been more than mid to high sixties standing in full sun.

What had come over him?

A twig snapped, and he swiveled to see Sadie standing a few feet away holding two paper to-go cups.

Her wide eyes glinted with surprise, maybe even a hint of trepidation.

She'd caught him watching Lucy, he was almost certain.

He prayed she couldn't read his mind. Or had his expression given enough away already?

Her features settled into a cautious smile as she spanned the short distance to stand beside him. "Here you go." She handed him one of the piping-hot beverages. "Lucy said she was meeting you here."

"Thanks," he rasped, clearing his throat before taking a sip.

The sweet and spicy cider packed a lot of heat, and he hoped it didn't accentuate his already blazing face and neck.

He needed to get ahold of himself. But he couldn't help feeling exposed, somehow, as though Sadie had seen too much.

"Between you and me," she said in a conspiratorial tone, "I'm hoping she'll fall in love with one of them and it'll convince her to stay."

"What do you mean?" His pulse faltered. "Is she going somewhere?"

Sadie shot him a curious glance. "Being in Poppy Creek was always supposed to be temporary. She came back to help with the renovation of the inn. Now that it's finally open..." She trailed off, but Vick didn't need her to finish her thought.

Lucy's job was done. She'd be moving on to something else soon.

All this time, he'd been worried about his plans to leave town, about leaving her behind. When all along, she never intended to stay.

Why hadn't he realized that before?

And more importantly, why did it bother him so much?

~

When Lucy finally extricated herself from the pile of puppies, she had the hardest time saying goodbye to the chubby ball of sunshine she guessed to be part golden Labrador. But what would she do with a dog when she had no idea where she'd wind up next?

After a prolonged snuggle, she patted the pup on the head and maneuvered through the swarm of cuteness to join Vick and Sadie.

For a moment, it seemed like she'd interrupted something, but before she had a chance to find out, Sadie handed her a cup of apple cider and excused herself, heading back to her booth.

"Looks like you made a new friend." Vick nodded toward the pen, and Lucy turned to follow his gaze.

The roly-poly pup pressed her face up to the fence, wiggling her bottom in hopes that she'd come back.

"Oh, she's breaking my heart." Lucy pressed a hand to her chest, surprised by the not-so-subtle ache. She'd always loved dogs, and adored babysitting Fitz, but having her own just didn't seem possible right now.

"What's stopping you from adopting her?" His tone held a twinge of something more than casual curiosity, but she couldn't quite place it.

"Life, I guess." Suddenly somber, she sipped her cider, trying not to glance behind her. She couldn't bear to see those big, pleading brown eyes again. Not after part of her already felt like she'd left a piece of her heart behind in that pen.

How could she explain life's complications to a dog? It wasn't just that she might be moving soon. What if she adopted her, then her migraines got worse? What if she had a serious illness that required hospitalization?

As the melancholy thoughts spun in her mind, her throat tightened. She really didn't want to go down this road right now.

Vick must have sensed her shift in mood, because he asked, "Do you want to walk around a little or get something to eat before we start filming?"

"No, that's okay." She managed a smile, genuinely appreciating his considerate suggestion. "We can get started. I don't want to miss the pumpkin parachute contest."

They spent the next hour collecting enough footage for the video before following the most mouthwatering aroma to a booth serving warm *picarones con miel*—Peruvian doughnuts made with pumpkin puree and topped with a fragrant anise and bay leaf infused honey glaze. Armed with two each, they joined the crowd eagerly awaiting the pumpkin parachute competition.

Townspeople gathered on either side of a small field blocked off by caution tape while contestants got in line behind a catapult specially designed for launching pumpkins.

Each contestant fastened a homemade parachute to their pumpkin, which would be hurled straight into the sky, with the goal of landing safely. Winners were chosen based on the degree of splatter. The most intact pumpkin won.

Of course, most of the audience came for the carnage, Lucy included. Even as an adult, she enjoyed the unusual entertainment.

"Who do you think will win?" Vick asked, licking the honey glaze off his fingers.

"Definitely Sammy." She pointed to a young boy at the end of the line.

"Really?" He didn't look convinced. "My money's on that guy."

He gestured toward Brent Jacobs, a high school senior who had a reputation for elaborate, and often high-tech, pranks and shenanigans.

Not a bad guess, but Lucy had the inside track. Sammy went to school with Eliza's son, Ben, and she raved about what a whiz he was at both science and math. Lucy was pretty sure she'd used the word *prodigy* to describe the scrawny kid with spiky blue hair and braces.

She was about to tell Vick, when he said, "Care to make things interesting?"

"What did you have in mind?" Something in his expression—both playful and nervous—piqued her curiosity.

"How about a wager? If your guy wins, I'll buy you dinner tonight. Anywhere you want."

Lucy blinked, convinced she'd misheard. Did he really say dinner? And anywhere she wanted?

She immediately pictured a cozy little café in Primrose Valley, the one with fancy linens and candles on every tabletop. It would be both charming and very, very private.

"Unless you're not confident in your choice," he added when she didn't respond.

So, she hadn't been dreaming after all. She swallowed the lump of excitement and uncertainty lodged in her throat. "And what if you win?"

He considered this a moment, and said, "Then I guess you're buying me dinner."

He grinned, and Lucy barely refrained from cheering out loud.

Win or lose, they'd have dinner together. *Tonight.* Was this really happening?

"Deal." Without thinking, she stuck out her hand to shake on it.

His warm, rough palm closed around hers, and the contact made her momentarily light-headed.

She caught herself before she visibly swayed and retracted her hand from his firm, all-too-intimate grasp.

For the next several minutes, they watched the pumpkins soar into the air and plummet back to earth, smashing against the dirt in an explosion of orange goo and projectile pumpkin seeds. More onlookers arrived, jostling them together in the commotion and excitement. Each time their arms grazed or their shoulders bumped, she forgot how to breathe, which only made her feel woozier.

Yeesh. Get a hold of yourself.

She wasn't usually the swoony type.

As the sun beat down on them, she wished she'd brought a bottle of water. Dehydration had set in.

By the time Sammy stepped up to the catapult, his tiny frame looked like a distant blur.

Black spots started to form in front of her eyes, and panic gripped her.

Please, no...

Not here. Not now.

The dull pressure lurking in the background grew to a steady throb, escalating more quickly than it ever had before.

Keep it together.

She gritted her teeth, determined to hold the migraine at bay.

But a sharp, piercing dagger stabbed her left temple, catching her off guard.

Instinctively, she pressed a hand to the side of her head, as though she could squash the pain with her palm.

Please, please, not here, she silently whimpered, on the verge of tears as all her long-hoped-for plans slipped through her fingers.

Sucking in a shallow breath, she searched the distorted figures around her for a way out, and prayed for enough strength to disappear without being noticed.

But the ground seemed to tilt beneath her feet.

She wasn't sure whether it happened within a few minutes or

mere seconds, but a strong, steady hand wrapped around her waist, and she finally closed her eyes, desperate for relief.

CHAPTER 14

Fear surged through Vick's body as he led Lucy away from the boisterous crowd.

What happened? One minute, she was fine, the next, she could barely stand.

Pain creased her forehead and although her eyes were scrunched shut, her lashes were damp.

He had one arm slung around her waist, leading her toward the house so she could lie down.

While they walked—and he half carried her—his brain ran through a plan of action, including the possibility of calling 911, even if she protested.

So far, she'd insisted she'd be fine, although her voice warbled and all the blood had drained from her face.

He caught her wince again, and a single tear slipped down her cheek.

His chest twisted. He couldn't take it anymore.

Sweeping her off the ground, he cradled her in his arms.

He expected her to object, but she melted against him, leaning her head on his shoulder.

The fact that she'd consented to being carried intensified his concern.

Beads of sweat collected on his brow, and every muscle in his body clenched, anticipating the worst.

What was wrong with her?

He repeated a silent prayer, tormented by the thought that it might be something serious.

When they reached the silo, he strode through the front door and headed straight for his room.

He gently laid her on the twin bed, while she mumbled "I'm fine" over and over in a tone distorted by her palpable distress.

Clearly, she wasn't fine. And she wasn't going anywhere until he was assured of her health and safety.

He removed her boots and the purse strung over her shoulder and covered her with a throw blanket.

Hating to leave her, he hurried into the kitchen and returned a few minutes later with ibuprofen and a glass of water. It might not do much in her afflicted condition, but he had to try something.

Carefully supporting her neck, he helped her sit up and swallow the pills before easing her back on the pillow.

Next, he prepared a damp cloth for her forehead.

As he smoothed back her hair, he noticed her flinch against the sunlight streaming across her eyelids.

After draping the cool cloth on her too-warm skin, he quickly crossed to the window and yanked the drapes closed, plunging the room into dark shadows.

For a moment, he stood against the wall, his heart thundering against his rib cage as he observed her frail form lying there motionless.

He wiped his clammy palms against his jeans, trying to keep his fingers from shaking.

Now wasn't the time to panic.

He closed his eyes, focusing on his breathing, but the

haunting image of towering flames burned in his mind's eye. The deafening blast assaulted his eardrums, followed by strips of metal hitting the street.

Shouts, screams… the *screams*.

His eyelids rocketed open, his pulse racing out of control, careening over the edge.

Lucy needs you.

He inhaled, counting to seven as he tapped each finger against his thumb in practiced succession.

When his chest finally rose and fell in a normal rhythm, he dragged a chair by the bedside.

Losing track of time, he sat there for an hour or more, periodically dampening the cloth until she drifted off to sleep.

Finally, her breathing slowed.

While she slept, Vick never left her side, never stopped asking himself the same questions over and over.

Would she be okay?

And what would he do if she wasn't?

~

Lucy's eyelids fluttered open, and she slowly adjusted to the dim lighting.

Disoriented, she couldn't remember where she was or how long she'd been there.

Alarmed, she tried to sit upright, but her sluggish brain protested.

"Easy."

Vick.... She recognized his husky voice.

He propped a few pillows against the wooden headboard and helped her lean against them.

She gazed up at him, her eyes struggling to focus in the shadows.

His handsome features were twisted with worry. "How are you feeling?"

"Like I played chicken with a brick wall and lost." She attempted a wry smile, and some of the tension in his clenched muscles relaxed.

"Here. Drink this." He handed her a glass of cool water.

She gulped most of it down and passed it back to him. "Thank you."

He set it on the nightstand, then leaned forward, his forearms braced against his thighs. "What happened, Luce?"

Her heart trembled at the sound of her nickname rolling off his lips. He'd never called her that before.

It suddenly occurred to her that they were in his bedroom and he'd taken care of her during the last few hours. He'd been gentle and nurturing and… tender.

Her pulse stuttered again.

Was it possible Vick Johnson had real, tangible feelings for her?

Or were her fuzzy, addled thoughts playing tricks on her?

She tried to focus on his question. "It was a headache."

"I've never seen a headache like that before."

"Technically, I guess you'd call it a migraine. They're worse than a headache."

"What caused it?"

Lucy stared at her hands, realizing she'd twisted the edge of the throw blanket into a tangled knot.

Should she tell him about her doctor's appointment? She could still hear Dr. Dunlap recite all the potential causes, his voice faltering when he got to the most serious possibilities—the reason for the MRI.

She met his gaze. His dark-gray eyes glinted with apprehension, and she couldn't bring herself to tell him the truth.

Why worry him needlessly? There wasn't much point in both of them being overly concerned before she had any real answers.

She reached for the glass of water and took another sip before settling on a half-truth. "Probably a combination of too much sun, being on my feet all day, and dehydration." While all those reasons may not be the *root* cause, she had a feeling they'd contributed to the severity.

Her response seemed to ease some of his anxiety, and he straightened. "Are you hungry?"

"A little." She tried to hide her disappointment over missing their romantic dinner that evening.

"You stay here and rest, and I'll throw something on the barbecue." He grabbed her glass and stood. "First, I'll get you some more water. Do you want to keep the drapes closed?"

"Can you open them a smidge? Just to let in a little light, but not too much." Everything still ached, especially her eyes, but she wanted to be able to see him better.

"Sure thing." He pulled them back an inch, before returning to the kitchen for more water.

He set the full glass on the nightstand and cast one last wary glance in her direction before disappearing from sight.

In his absence, Lucy took the opportunity to study the oddly shaped room, looking for any insight it might offer into the man of mystery.

She spotted a hoodie draped over a high-backed chair, a stack of books on a worn leather trunk, and a compact weight rack set up against the wall.

No photos, letters, or postcards.

Zero personal mementos of any kind.

Besides the fact that he liked to work out and read, his bedroom told her very little about him. Other than what she already knew—he was extremely private and guarded.

Disappointed with her lack of new insight, she searched for something to occupy her time. Her purse—and hence, her cell phone—taunted her from across the room on the antique dresser. But she didn't feel well enough yet to attempt retrieving it on her own.

The books were also out of reach, not that she particularly cared for Westerns or legal thrillers.

What she wouldn't give for a romance novel or even the latest issue of *Vogue*.

She noticed a faded map on the nightstand beside her. Not the most riveting reading material, but it would do in a pinch. Besides, she didn't think Vick would mind her looking at something as impersonal as a roadmap of the United States.

She unfolded it across her lap, and immediately noticed the red circles drawn around several small towns, Poppy Creek among them.

Her gaze drifted to a tear in the upper left-hand corner near the state of Alaska. The city of Unalaska was circled in the same red ink as the others, and the words *Dutch Harbor* and *Lucky Lure* were handwritten in pencil beside it.

A floorboard creaked, and Lucy glanced up, her pulse spiking as though she'd been caught snooping.

Vick stood in the doorway with a plate of crackers and a magazine featuring national parks. "I, uh, thought you might like a light snack and something to look at while you wait for dinner." His gaze landed on the map, then flitted back to her face, his discomfort evident in the flex of his jaw.

"I'm so sorry." She rushed to refold the map, fumbling over the creases. "I was looking for something to occupy the time and didn't think—"

"It's fine," he cut in, sliding the plate onto the nightstand.

He hovered beside the bed, and a nervous energy sizzled through the room.

The cautious part of her brain said to leave things be, but her curiosity won out. "Are these all places you've lived before?" she asked, watching his expression closely.

"Most of them."

Something about the city in Alaska had stood out to her, and she wasn't sure why. On a hunch, she said, "Except for this one," and tapped near the torn edge. "This is where you're going next, isn't it?"

He nodded, shifting his feet.

Why wouldn't he look her in the eye?

"I've heard Alaska is beautiful." Somehow, her voice sounded calmer than she felt. "When do you leave?"

He parted his lips, but before he could respond, his phone beeped in his back pocket. Drawing it out, he turned off the timer. "I need to flip the steaks. I'll be right back."

As he strode out of the room, a sinking feeling settled in the pit of her stomach.

Whatever he'd been about to tell her, she wasn't going to like it.

CHAPTER 15

Vick set both dinner plates on the coffee table, grateful he'd learned a thing or two working at the diner. He'd managed to whip up two steaks, grilled zucchini and red onions, and barbecue cheesy potatoes.

By the time dinner was ready, Lucy felt well enough to sit upright and eat, but Vick thought she'd be more comfortable on the couch than the cramped kitchen table.

Okay, so it wasn't really a couch. It was more like a two-person loveseat, but he'd decided against using the more accurate term... for obvious reasons.

He feared his actions today already revealed his feelings for Lucy, without asking her to sit on symbolic furniture.

While he'd never doubted that he cared about her, he hadn't been willing to admit how much. The roller coaster of fear and finding out if she'd be okay had forced him to face a hard truth.

And he'd come to a surprising decision.

Lucy rested the plate on her knees, her lips quirked. "You cut my steak for me?"

"Yeah, I hope that's okay. I'm not trying to patronize you. I just figured it'd be easier to eat on the couch that way."

Her smile grew, bringing some color back to her face.

Man, it was good to see her smile again.

"That's very thoughtful. Thank you. It smells delicious."

After some brief small talk about recipes and grilling techniques, they savored each bite in companionable silence.

Tucked in the back of the property, they could still hear faint sounds of the festivities, but Vick didn't mind missing the rest of the events.

The only place he wanted to be was right here.

"You know," Lucy said thoughtfully, "I don't think I ever saw who won the pumpkin parachute contest."

"Your guy won. The pumpkin cracked up the middle, but didn't split." He hesitated, his heart thrumming, before adding, "So, I guess I owe you dinner."

"This doesn't count?" Lucy sounded surprised, but he also noticed a twinge of pleasure in her inflection, which gave him the courage he needed.

"Nope. You earned a meal in a real restaurant. Any place you want."

She smiled again, a full-on grin this time, before stuffing a forkful of cheesy potatoes in her mouth.

His chest swelled with an intoxicating mix of happiness and relief. Not only was her migraine a one-off, and not some serious ailment, she genuinely seemed interested in having dinner with him.

Time for phase two.

Setting down his fork, he gulped a few sips of water first, gathering courage.

Every rational voice inside his head screamed that he was making a mistake. Stick to the plan, they said. If you go through with this, you'll regret it.

But he was tired of listening to them. Tired of running. Tired of wondering what if?

"About your question earlier," he began, suppressing his

mental protests. "My plans to leave town aren't set in stone."

"Really?" Her fork paused midair, eyes wide yet cautious, as though she didn't dare get her hopes up.

He pushed forward, unsure how far he would go, how much he'd reveal. "I have a job lined up, but I'm not sure it's the right move for me."

Her hand drifted to her plate, but she didn't look away, her gaze questioning.

He was so close to telling her more, to confessing his growing feelings, but his self-preservation kicked in, shoving a thought into the forefront of his mind like a shield. "What about you? I heard you might be leaving soon."

For the first time, she broke eye contact, glancing at the floor.

His pulse faltered.

And he was no longer certain he wanted to hear her answer.

~

Lucy struggled to steady her nerves.

It was happening.

The moment she'd longed for—open communication about the future.

But even in her excitement, apprehension slithered around her heart, hissing an unwelcome reminder of her dim reality.

How could she pursue something with Vick when she couldn't even confront her own fate?

"My plans aren't set in stone, either," she said softly, daring to meet his gaze again.

Her heart soared at the glimmer of hope in his eyes.

Now more than ever, she agonized over the tug-of-war between discovering the truth about her condition and the need to protect her bubble of blissful idealism.

But deep beneath the shiny surface of optimism, she feared what would happen if the bubble burst.

"I guess we're both playing things by ear, then." His voice carried a hint of hesitation, as though he didn't know what to say next.

Truthfully, neither did she. It felt like they were standing on the edge of a precipice, but she wasn't sure if either of them had a parachute.

Either way, if they jumped, they may end up like the pile of smashed pumpkins from earlier.

She smiled for lack of anything better to say.

"Ready for dessert?" Vick stood and cleared the dinner plates.

"What'd you have in mind?"

"I have a weakness for Eliza's caramel pecan espresso bars, but they have caffeine, if you'd rather not have any this late in the day."

"I don't mind. They sound amazing and the caffeine should help with the aftereffects of the migraine." A dull throb lingered inside her head and a thick fog weighed down her thoughts, which was the worst timing considering the intense nature of their conversation.

While he rummaged around the kitchen, Lucy pulled the blanket tighter around her legs. As dusk fell, the air grew noticeably colder. Wind howled through the trees, mingling with the hum of farm animals settling in for the night.

Vick returned with a pastry box full of the most decadent-looking dessert bars and two steaming mugs of spiced apple cider.

Before sitting down, he turned on a small space heater in the corner of the room.

Lucy eyed the potbelly stove, thinking it would be the perfect addition to the idyllic setting. "Do you ever use the fireplace?"

"No." The single syllable sounded stiff, almost defensive.

How strange. She'd never met anyone who didn't prefer the warm glow of flickering flames or the scent of burning logs. "Any particular reason?"

Before he could answer, there was a knock at the door. Although, the noise came from somewhere near the bottom of the frame, which was odd.

Vick set down his mug, a knowing smile on his lips, as though he anticipated their guest.

Lucy buried her disappointment at the interruption of their cozy, intimate evening.

"Hey, Buddy," Vick said in greeting, and a miniature goat trotted across the threshold.

He made a beeline for Lucy, wagging his short, stubby tail in introduction.

"Well, hello there." She laughed, setting down her mug as the goat nuzzled her leg in a shameless ploy for head scratches.

"I see how it is," Vick said with a playful grumble, rejoining her on the couch. "There's a pretty girl in the room and suddenly I'm invisible."

Her heart somersaulted. She'd been called a lot of things in her life, from stunning to breathtaking to gorgeous, but hearing something as simple as *pretty* come out of Vick's mouth topped all the other compliments combined.

She tried to moderate the thrill in her voice when she asked, "I take it he's a frequent houseguest?"

"Buddy stops by every day, usually more than once, and almost always when I have food."

"He's adorable." She scratched his chin this time, becoming fast friends.

"You appear to be his new favorite person. Did you have pets growing up?"

"Sadly, no. I've always wanted a dog, but Mom and Dad had a hard enough time raising six kids. What about you?"

"Not officially. But we had a house mouse for a while that hung out in the bottom cabinets of our kitchen. Mom used to talk to her like she was one of the family." A softness stole over his features, and the happy mood shifted.

"You and your mom were close?" she asked gently.

"Yeah." His voice sounded far away, and something in his inflection told her not to press.

He cleared his throat. "What about you? Are you close with your mom?"

"Yes, although we frequently butt heads."

"About?"

"All sorts of things. Mostly over her aspirations for my life that aren't anything like my own." Although she found the constant unsolicited advice tiresome, she knew her mother meant well. After struggling to make ends meet most of her life, Elaine Gardener valued security above all else, especially for her only daughter.

"And what *are* your aspirations?" Vick asked, his curiosity palpable.

Petting Buddy with one hand, she lifted her mug with the other, inhaling the sweet, spicy aroma of Vick's homemade cider.

She took a sip, stalling while she scoured her brain for an appropriate response. Even without the grogginess from the migraine, she knew she wouldn't find one. Finally, she released a heavy sigh. "Honestly, I have no idea. I was an art major and studied set design, thinking I might work in Hollywood or maybe on Broadway in New York."

"You changed your mind?"

"I guess. Although, it wasn't that intentional. I'm not sure I had the drive or passion to fully pursue it. Then, when my parents wanted me to join the family business, I didn't have a reason to say no."

"And now?"

"Now..." She trailed off, desperate for the answer to materialize on the tip of her tongue. Per usual, none came.

"I don't know what I want to do. But I'd like it to be something meaningful." Her thoughts drifted to Jayla and her selfless job traveling the country helping others. Maybe she should consider something similar?

"What about your YouTube channel?"

"Oh, that's just a hobby," she said quickly. "Nothing serious."

"Could it be something serious?"

"Definitely not." She internally cringed at the idea. While she had fun with it for now, she could never take the so-called social media influencers seriously. And she didn't want to be lumped in with the vain look-at-me crowd.

No, she'd have to find something else to do with her life.

For now, she'd add her career to her long list of uncertainties.

Along with her health concerns and whatever was happening between her and Vick.

CHAPTER 16

As Lucy pushed through the front door of Sadie's Sweet Shop, the welcoming scent of caramelized sugar and rich, buttery chocolate swirled around her, evoking memories of her childhood.

She'd loved coming here as a young girl. And not simply because of the delectable sweets. Sadie's grandmother, Brigitte "Gigi" Durand, treated Lucy like a second granddaughter, arranging elaborate tea parties for them in the small courtyard behind the shop and teaching them all her tricks, like how to pull taffy and expertly dip caramel apples. She also knew Lucy's parents couldn't afford luxuries like artisan chocolates and other special confections, and frequently sent boxes home with her, claiming the batch "didn't turn out quite right."

"Hi!" Sadie waved from behind the counter, wearing her long red apron with the store's name printed across the front in swirly letters.

When Gigi opened the shop over twenty years ago, she named it after Sadie, her only grandchild, and bequeathed it to her on her eighteenth birthday. Some people thought Sadie was too young to handle so much responsibility, but Gigi had practically raised Sadie in the shop after her parents died. Plus, the fiery, globe-trotting eighty-six-year-old still helped Sadie run the place in between her jaunts to Italy, New Zealand, and most recently, Costa Rica.

"Those look good." Lucy eyed the small, round chocolates as Sadie scooped them into a glass jar.

"You have to try one." Sadie dropped a few into her palm.

"What are they?"

"Chocolate covered coffee beans. Gigi never cared for them until she tried them in Costa Rica. Apparently, the right coffee makes a huge difference."

"And we know where to find that." Lucy grinned and popped one in her mouth. The sweet chocolate perfectly balanced the earthiness of the coffee, while the combination of creaminess and crunch created a tantalizing mouthfeel. She promptly ate another one.

Sadie beamed. "I'm so glad you like them. Cassie wants to sell them on her website. And, of course, Gram loves the idea. They've already started brainstorming a catchy name." With an amused shake of her head, she turned toward the back counter and poured two cups of hot chocolate from an antique silver chocolate pot. If Lucy remembered correctly, Gigi found the treasure on a trip to Bavaria over a decade ago.

Choosing their usual spot at the corner window, Sadie set the mugs on one of the several tabletops painted to resemble an old-fashioned candy. They always gravitated toward the round peppermint with a white center and red stripes on the side. Gigi said it was because they were both sweet and bold, a comparison that still made her smile.

Seated next to the window pane, Lucy felt the chill of the early morning air seep through the glass and warmed her hands on the toasty ceramic mug, savoring the aromatic steam swirling above the rim.

"How long did you stay at the event yesterday?" Sadie asked, settling onto the chair across from her. "I wanted to say goodbye before I left, but couldn't find you anywhere."

Lucy filled her in on the unexpected migraine, leaving off the part about the chronic occurrence. While she loved her friend dearly and confided in her about most things, she wasn't ready to divulge her ailment to anyone yet, not even her closest friends and family. At least, not until she knew more about it, which would require finally making the appointment with the specialist.

"I'm so sorry!" Sadie said with genuine concern. "How are you feeling now?"

"Much better. Tired and a little foggy headed, but these are helping." She grinned and tossed another chocolate covered coffee bean in her mouth.

"I'll be sure to add that to the marketing material," Sadie teased.

"Is Gigi here today?" Lucy glanced at the long rectangular window that separated the main part of the shop from the demonstration room where they taught candy-making classes.

"No, she has book club, but don't change the subject."

"What do you mean?" Lucy feigned innocence, hiding behind a sip of hot chocolate.

"I need to hear more about how Vick *carried* you into his house and took care of you until you were feeling better."

"And cooked dinner," Lucy added with a blush.

"That settles it. The man is close to perfect."

Flustered, Lucy dropped her gaze to the velvety liquid, studying the creamy swirls on the surface, her heart thrumming. "He might not be leaving town after all."

"Really? He actually said that?" Sadie's tone held a hint of skepticism.

Lucy shared the details of her conversation with Vick, adding their plans to have dinner later that week, once he was back on the lunch shift.

"And how do you feel about it?" Sadie asked, observing her closely.

"Nervous. Excited. Terrified." She toyed with the swooping handle, glancing over her shoulder to make sure no one had slipped inside and could overhear them.

"I've never seen you get like this over a guy before."

"This one is different, Sade. I can't really explain it. He's so... *admirable*, which might sound cheesy. But with five older brothers, I've always had solid role models. And I know they'd all be proud to have Vick in the family. Especially Jack, who already loves him."

"Wow," Sadie breathed, trying to wrap her head around the admission. Meeting her gaze, she asked softly, "Do *you* love him?"

Heat blazed up Lucy's neck, threatening to splash across her cheeks. *Love* was such a loaded word. And yet, she didn't balk as much as she'd expected. Was it possible her feelings for Vick ran that deep? "I don't know," she said at last, trying to read the flutter in her stomach. "Maybe. The past several months, I've admired and respected him from afar, but lately..."

How could she explain the jumble of emotions? The last few days, she'd observed a depth to Vick she knew existed but wasn't sure she'd ever get to see for herself. But he'd actually let her in, past his protective walls, which only made her fall harder.

She realized her lips had arched into a smile, and she took a self-conscious sip of hot chocolate, embarrassed to be so smitten.

"I'm happy for you, Luce." Sadie sounded sincere, but a subtle wariness lurked behind her words. "Just... be careful, okay? In case he doesn't stay after all, I don't want you to get hurt."

"I will," Lucy assured her.

Although, deep down, she knew it was already too late for that.

~

Vick absentmindedly sliced a chunk of apple and tossed it to Buddy, who'd benefited from his lack of appetite that morning.

He'd barely touched his coffee, too lost in his thoughts. He wasn't sure how he'd get through the next few days until dinner with Lucy. It was all he could think about.

Although, he still wasn't sure what he was doing. He had solid reasons for never getting close to anyone, and his boundaries had served him well over the years. This was the first time he'd considered breaking his long-held rules.

What if he was making a mistake?

His phone buzzed in his cargo pants pocket, snapping him out of his reverie.

"Hey, Colt."

"Hey, I hate to do this to you, but I need a favor."

"Sure. What's up?"

"I promised Frank I'd help him roast today, since all the guests had activities lined up elsewhere. But one of them had a change in plans, and I can't get away. Can you cover for me? I heard you've helped Frank before."

"Yeah, I can do it." He'd appreciate the distraction.

"Thanks, man. I owe you one."

After ending the call, Vick sliced the rest of the apple and set it on the porch. "It's all yours, Bud." He patted him on the head before ducking inside to grab a few things.

Unsure how long he'd be gone, he lobbed a protein bar and water bottle in the back seat, adding a jacket at the last minute in case it rained.

The entire ride to Frank's place, his excitement grew. He'd had a blast helping last time, and reading Frank's book had only increased his interest in the unique roasting method. It would be fascinating to experience it again but armed with his newfound knowledge.

He rolled to a stop in the gravel driveway, and immediately spotted the smoke billowing from behind the house. Frank didn't earn any points for patience, given he'd only arrived five minutes past the time Colt was supposed to be here.

As he rounded the corner, he expected Frank to be surprised. Colt hadn't mentioned giving him a heads-up about the switch. But Frank didn't even raise one bushy eyebrow and simply waved him over.

For the next twenty minutes, the gruff taskmaster leaned against his smooth manzanita cane and barked orders. When they'd finished, and the coffee was left to cool in the glass mason jars, Vick grinned, once again completely exhilarated by the process.

"Why are you smiling?" Frank grunted. "We're not done." Using his cane, he pointed to a large barrel of green coffee beans. "Fill the bucket with three scoops of Costa Rica, three Sumatra, and four Kenya. I'll show you how to load the machine. Try not to muck it up."

They went through the entire roasting routine four times before Frank sanctioned a break.

"How much coffee have we roasted?" Vick drained a large gulp from his water bottle, beads of sweat scattered across his brow despite the cool breeze.

"Enough to supply the businesses around town. But we still need to put together the donation for the veterans shelter. Got any gas left in the tank?"

"Yes, sir." He straightened and set aside the water bottle, ready to get back to work.

Frank studied him a moment, then shuffled toward the house without saying a word.

Vick stared after him, unsure if he should follow. "Want me to finish up here?" He was fairly confident he could get through a roast on his own.

"Lunch first," Frank called over his shoulder.

Still stumped, Vick didn't budge. That wasn't exactly a definitive answer. Was he supposed to join him?

As if reading his mind, Frank added, "Bevy left a pastrami on rye, which is enough for two if we supplement with pie."

Vick thought about the protein bar he'd left in the Jeep, deciding Frank's offer sounded better. He followed him through the back door into the modest kitchen.

Frank pulled a sandwich from the fridge and divided the two halves onto separate plates. "Can you make a decent cup of coffee?"

"Yes, sir."

Frank nodded toward a jar of coffee beans, then busied himself with slicing the mulberry pie.

Vick took a moment to survey his options. He noticed a French press, espresso machine, automatic drip coffeepot, and an AeroPress. Going with his gut, he chose a tried-and-true method he'd perfected during his time in the Marines and grabbed a small saucepan.

After grinding the beans into a fine powder, he dumped them in the saucepan, then added water. Placing the pan on the stove, he boiled the mixture until the coffee settled on the bottom. His marine buddies called his concoction A Mug of Mud, but they'd lapped it up.

Vick poured two cups and brought them to the table where Frank waited.

Frank eyed it suspiciously, then slurped.

Vick gauged his reaction, observing every micro-expression, counting it a win when he didn't spit it out.

"Not bad. Although, I don't usually drink my coffee with a spoon." The old man's eyes twinkled, and Vick took it as a compliment.

"I enjoyed your book," Vick told him before taking a bite of the towering stack of thick bread and generous deli meat. The sharp flavor of pastrami and rye melded with the sweet pickles and lemon-basil mayo. Beverly sure knew how to make a sandwich.

"It's all right. But the second one is better, thanks to Cassie. I'll give you a copy before you leave."

Vick didn't mention he'd already ordered one to be shipped. Frank's two books, and his mother's worn copy of *Peter Pan and Wendy,* were the only reading material he'd planned to take with him when he left.

That is, before he'd decided to stay and turned down the position on the *Lucky Lure.*

The familiar wave of apprehension washed over him. What would he do with himself now? Jack would probably let him keep his job at the diner, but is that what he wanted?

Before he realized he was speaking out loud, he said, "I think it's great you're able to do something you love. Most people aren't that lucky." He thought about his mother and her abandoned dreams of becoming America's next sweetheart. Instead, she'd worked dead-end jobs that paid next to nothing, with little thanks let alone accolades.

He'd only ever had one calling—the Marines—and that had been taken from him. Now, it didn't matter what he did with his life. Work was simply a means to an end, a paycheck to keep the lights on.

Frank took another sip of coffee, his peppery brows knit together. "Someone once said, 'It's not in doing what you like, but in liking what you do' that's the key."

"What does that mean?" Vick asked, easily put off by empty platitudes.

"The job itself isn't usually what matters the most, but how you show up to it."

Vick still wasn't sure what he meant, but it had given him something to think about.

CHAPTER 17

The next few days flew by in a whirlwind for Lucy. Her YouTube channel had grown beyond her wildest expectations, and the fall video series had reaped unexpected benefits for all of the nonprofits she'd highlighted, not to mention the inn.

But the biggest blessing of the week, by far, had been dinner with Vick. The events of the evening had unfolded even better than she'd imagined.

Tearing her gaze from the road, she stole a glance at his profile. His strong features were illuminated in the soft moonlight filtering through the windows of her Mercedes.

Something in the air had shifted ever since their dinner date a couple of nights ago. They'd talked for hours in the intimate café in Primrose Valley, prolonging the meal with dessert followed by cappuccinos. When it came time for the restaurant to close, they'd continued their conversation in the Jeep with the heater running.

Looking back, Lucy realized they hadn't discussed anything particularly deep or profound. In fact, most of the topics were rather lighthearted and inconsequential, but something about the casual exchange lent an easy familiarity to their relationship that Lucy relished. She could see herself spending every evening with Vick, chatting about books and their favorite hobbies, sharing silly anecdotes and childhood memories.

Sadie had advised her to be careful, to not get too far ahead of herself. But she couldn't help it. Things with Vick were going too well not to let go and live in the moment.

She was especially looking forward to tonight's event—Hitchcock & Hayrides—organized by the arts council and held at the Sterling Rose Estate. They were meeting up with the entire group: Sadie, Jack and Kat, Reed and Olivia, Luke and Cassie, Grant and Eliza, and Colt and Penny.

Plus, Kat had invited all the guests at the inn to join them, which meant she might have another opportunity to connect Landon and Sadie. Perhaps if Sadie could experience the same intoxicating flutter in her stomach, she'd understand why Lucy couldn't be cautious when it came to her feelings for Vick.

At the very least, Sadie would see them interact tonight and be assured that Lucy wasn't fabricating their connection. There was definitely something going on between them. She tucked the knowledge in her heart for safekeeping as she pulled into the crowded parking lot.

Vick grabbed their blanket and pillows from the back seat and led the way toward the pathway that meandered up the hill. Lucy followed close behind, her pulse thrumming with anticipation.

When they reached the top, she drew in a breath, blown away by the stunning sight.

Thin strands of twinkling lights stretched across the lawn like a soiree of frolicking fairies. Beneath the glittering glow, townspeople gathered on blankets and in rows of folding chairs facing the enormous red barn where a projector cast the opening credits of *To Catch a Thief* starring Cary Grant and Grace Kelly.

"Lucy! Vick! Over here!" Cassie waved from the center of the throng, and they wove their way toward the group. The only faces missing were Landon and Morgan, which gave Lucy pause.

"We saved you a spot over there." Olivia pointed beside Sadie and Jayla's blanket. "But before the film starts, help yourself to hot chocolate and popcorn."

Lucy followed her gaze toward an adorable self-serve snack station featuring a vintage popcorn machine reminiscent of old-time movie theaters.

"I'll get it," Vick offered once he'd arranged the blanket and pillows on the soft grass.

Lucy smiled, watching him maneuver his way through the crowd.

Although he wore the camera on a strap around his neck, they'd both forgotten to take a single photo since they arrived. Almost as if the videos had taken a back seat to spending time together. As much as she loved the thought, she didn't want to let Jack and Kat down, so she took off after him, hoping to record some footage before the movie started.

As she passed the last row of folding chairs, she noticed Landon and Morgan sitting next to each other. While Morgan looked perfectly content, Landon kept craning his neck, trying to glimpse their group over the tops of people's heads.

Lucy bit back a sigh of disappointment. She'd met women like Morgan before, natural-born manipulators. But Landon needed to man up. If he couldn't handle Morgan, he wasn't the right match for Sadie, who needed someone assertive.

Her heart warmed as she approached Vick at the snack stand.

On paper, they weren't an obvious couple, either.

But much like her brother and Kat, they brought out the best in each other.

And although she barely dared to put her wish into words, she hoped tonight might finally lead to their first kiss.

~

As they all milled about afterward, discussing their favorite scenes in the movie, Vick realized he didn't remember a single thing about it. He'd been too distracted by Lucy lying next to him on the blanket to pay attention. Every time she shifted position, her arm grazed his. And even through the thick fabric of their coats, his skin sizzled.

A dozen or more times, he'd been tempted to slide his arm around her and pull her close. His need to be near her, to touch her, had become difficult to ignore. But he didn't want their first real show of affection to be in front of other people.

How would he get her alone?

"Time for the hayride! Before it gets too crowded." Cassie clapped her hands in excitement, and the group headed for the orchard at the bottom of the hill.

Lucy stumbled on the dimly lit trail, and Vick steadied her with a gentle hand on her lower back. Heat surged up his arm again, despite the chilly night air. His heavy tactical jacket suddenly seemed like overkill.

When they arrived at the bottom, Vick spotted horse-drawn wagons padded with hay bales. He'd never heard of a hayride after dark and was curious to see what Olivia had planned.

They split up into three pairs per wagon.

Vick helped Lucy climb inside, and his heart nearly burst when she sat so close beside him, their knees touched. He was grateful when Luke and Cassie and Grant and Eliza sat toward the front of the wagon, giving them a modicum of privacy in the back.

As they headed deeper into the rows of apple trees, the branches blocked out some of the moonlight. The darkness combined with the gentle clip-clop of hooves on the ground would've been enough to lull him to sleep if his pulse wasn't working overtime in such intimate proximity to Lucy. Her heady perfume whirled around him, making it hard to keep his hands to himself.

What if he slowly slipped his arm around her shoulders?

Before he had a chance, Lucy gasped, drawing his focus straight ahead.

Glowing luminaries lined the pathway, guiding them toward what looked like a portal to a magical world. Flickering candles in glass votives and brass and pewter lanterns hung from the branches while amber string lights swirled through the treetops like a canopy of fiery stars.

"Have you ever seen anything so beautiful?" Lucy whispered.

Vick glanced down, momentarily captivated by the reflection of light in her luminous eyes.

The instant he'd met Lucy, he'd been struck by her beauty. It was impossible not to be. But the more he got to know her, the more he realized her beauty went far beyond her outward appearance. Her passion for life radiated like the sun, warming everything she touched. And her infectious joy had awakened parts of himself he'd kept dormant for years.

He could fight it all he wanted, but it wouldn't change facts. He'd fallen for Lucy Gardener. And he wanted to go all in.

When he didn't respond, she tilted her chin and met his gaze.

His thoughts must have been written on his face, because her breath caught, attracting his attention to her lips. His pulse stilled.

There was the kiss, perfectly conspicuous in the right-hand corner.

Without thinking, he lightly grazed her cheekbone with his fingertips, slowly tracing a pathway along the soft curve.

A fire kindled in her eyes at his touch.

His heart hammering, he leaned down, driven by a need unlike anything he'd ever felt before.

But before their lips met, the wheels of the wagon rolled over a rut, lurching them forward.

And broke the spell.

CHAPTER 18

Ever since the evening of the hayride, Lucy hadn't stopped daydreaming about their almost-kiss.

The only thing that had abated her disappointment in that moment was when Vick had asked her on an official date... sort of. While they already had plans to create a video featuring the Library Benefit Banquet, Vick had suggested they not only go together, but wear a couple's costume, since all the guests were supposed to come dressed as their favorite literary character. His idea for their costume had been the most telling, and she could hardly wait for the big night.

Unbelievable as it seemed, things between her and Vick were finally falling into place. Except for one tiny detail. If she stayed in Poppy Creek, she'd need a job.

Shoulders back, she strode through the double doors of the inn, eager to talk to Kat. While working at the inn wasn't her dream career, she knew Kat could use the help, especially since they were booking up quickly.

Speaking of bookings, Kat appeared to be checking in a new guest. Lucy didn't recognize the twentysomething woman with ink-black hair pulled into a loose ponytail down her back.

"Lucy!" Kat waved her over. "I'd like you to meet Hana Lee."

"Hi, Hana. It's nice to meet you." Lucy shook the woman's hand, smiling warmly.

They exchanged a few pleasantries, and Lucy tried to stay present in the conversation, but her focus kept drifting. She couldn't wait to discuss work opportunities with Kat and have at least one thing in her life settled. Plus, she assumed Kat would be thrilled if she took over some of the main duties and lightened her burden.

"How long will you be staying with us?" Lucy asked in her best innkeeper tone.

"Oh, well..." Hana turned to Kat as though seeking permission to respond.

"Permanently." Kat beamed. "I've hired her to help me run the inn."

"You did?" Lucy fought to keep the surprise and disappointment out of her voice.

"I started searching some hiring sites a while ago," Kat confessed. "But then we decided to keep our staff as small as possible until business picked up. Thanks to your videos, that happened sooner than we expected. And luckily, Hana was still available."

"I'd almost accepted a management position at a prominent hotel chain, but when Kat called and told me about Poppy Creek, it was an easy decision."

The two women continued to smile like all their dreams had come true, but Lucy struggled to mirror their delight. Now, she was back at square one with zero ideas. "That's so great." She finally managed a semblance of a smile, albeit faint.

"Did you stop by for something?" Kat asked. "I was about to give Hana the grand tour."

"Nothing important. I need to grab a few things in town. Can I get you anything?"

"Colt just made a run, so I think we're good. But thanks for checking."

After a brief goodbye, Lucy slipped outside, relishing the crisp air on her heated cheeks. A few minutes ago, the world seemed bright and cheerful.

Now, storm clouds rolled in, literally and figuratively.

She gazed up at the hazy sky and thick blanket of dreary gray blocking out the sun.

What would she do now?

Her only plan had failed before it ever began.

Seated in her Mercedes, she rolled down the convertible top. The wind in her hair always lifted her spirits and by the look of the clouds, the downpour wouldn't start for another hour, at least.

She zipped along the winding mountain road toward town, savoring the musky scent of impending rain as she mulled over other possibilities.

Between Gigi and the two high schoolers who worked part-time, Sadie didn't need help at the sweet shop. And the café seemed fully staffed as well, not that she really cared to be a barista.

What *did* she care about?

She'd asked herself that exact question for weeks. Simply knowing she wanted to make a difference in the world wasn't enough. She needed direction. Or more preferably, a neon sign from above.

Lost and discouraged, she pulled into a parking spot in front of the library and secured the canvas convertible top.

Maybe there was a book titled *Finding Your Life's Purpose for Dummies.*

When she walked inside, she collided with a frazzled-looking Beverly.

"Is everything all right?" Lucy asked.

"Oh, Lucy. Your timing is impeccable. I hate to ask, dear, but I need another favor."

"Anything. I'm happy to help."

"I placed an order for the diner's lunch special, and I was going to drive it over to Frank on my break, but my volunteer for story hour got a head cold, so I have to step in. Would you mind taking it to him for me? You don't have to stay, although I know he enjoyed your company last time."

Lucy smiled, grateful to feel needed. "I'd love to be Frank's lunch date. When will his order be ready?"

"It should be ready now, if you're not busy."

"Not at all." Her mood lighter, Lucy crossed the town square with a sense of purpose. At least, for the next hour or so. She'd have to sort out the rest of her life later.

She also couldn't restrain her excitement over the possibility of seeing Vick at work. Every minute spent with him elevated her entire day to a whole new level.

As she reached the entrance to the diner, the front door swung open.

Vick stepped out looking surprised to see her, but his features quickly settled into a smoldering smile that made her stomach swirl.

"Hi, Luce."

"Hi." Her throat dry, she did her best to swallow. She sure could get used to hearing him say her name like that. "Beverly asked me to deliver Frank's lunch again."

"I'll come with you. I'm just getting off my shift." He held the door open for her, and she ducked inside, loving that he felt comfortable enough to invite himself along.

If things continued to progress this smoothly, she'd be bringing Vick home for the holidays.

The thought made her shiver with happiness.

And she couldn't help wondering if he fantasized about their future, too.

~

The offer to accompany Lucy to Frank's had slipped out before Vick realized what he was saying. And although it startled him, he didn't regret it. It had been a long time since he'd felt that relaxed around someone, and he was learning to appreciate the shift in his status quo.

They ordered two more lunch specials—a tri-tip sandwich, baked zucchini chips, and an ice-cold bottle of sarsaparilla—and headed back outside.

"I parked over there." Lucy gestured across the town square.

"I'm right here. I'll drive." He held open the passenger door of the Jeep and waited for her to get situated before striding around to the other side.

She manually rolled down the window and sniffed the air. "Don't you love the smell before it rains?"

He couldn't help but smile at her enthusiasm. There was so much about life that Lucy loved. He'd come to admire that about her.

Before he could respond, she added, "And don't tell me it's because something is decaying."

He chuckled. "And what if it's true?"

"Then I especially don't want you to tell me," she teased as he climbed into the driver's seat.

As they drove to Frank's, he struggled to keep his eyes on the road. He enjoyed watching the wind whip her silky hair around her face, and her luminous smile more than made up for the lack of visible sun.

Whenever she glanced in his direction, his gaze drifted to the right-hand corner of her mouth. He'd come so close to capturing her elusive kiss the other night. Then the upset of the wagon had ignited chatter and laughter from the other couples, which ruined the intimate mood.

He couldn't wait for a second chance. Symbolically, the

Library Benefit Banquet would be the perfect opportunity. The night he'd originally planned to leave town would become the moment he told Lucy how he felt about her.

When he parked in the driveway, he immediately noticed the black cloud billowing behind the house. It looked thicker and darker than usual.

"Oh, Frank." Lucy gave a reproving shake of her head. "He's so stubborn. I'm positive he's not supposed to be roasting without help."

An uneasy feeling settled in Vick's stomach as they exited the Jeep.

The air smelled sharp and acrid, unlike the usual earthiness of roasting coffee.

As they rounded the back of the house, the smoke hit them first—thick and suffocating.

Vick saw the flames next, licking the roof of the barn.

He froze. Sweat slicked his palms. His heart lodged in his throat.

Time rewound, flinging him down a tunnel of repressed memories.

A fire blazed. Chunks of metal spewed into the sky like shrapnel.

The screams... the screams echoed in his eardrums.

Only now, they sounded like a woman's cries.

Lucy!

Lurching back to the present, he saw Lucy rush toward the burning building, shouting Frank's name.

Propelled by something outside of himself, he grabbed her arm and jerked her backward. "Stay here. And call 911."

Tears streamed down her pale face, but she nodded and scrambled for her phone.

Kneeling in the dirt where she'd dropped the to-go bag, he reached inside and pulled out the bottle of sarsaparilla. He twisted off the top and doused the front of his shirt before yanking the collar over his nose.

The first time he inhaled, his nostrils burned, but he barely noticed.

Heart pounding, he pushed through the dense fumes, squinting as they stung his eyes. His muscles tensed the second he saw Frank's body crumpled on the ground, and it took all of his self-control to rush past him.

He zeroed in on the roasting machine—the impetus of the fire. So far, the flames seemed contained to the roof. But left unchecked, the entire building could explode in an instant.

As he blindly searched for the off switch, images flashed in his mind's eye, leaving him disoriented.

Sand. Scorching Sun. A ramshackle village. A battered SUV. No license plate. His buddy Hodge up ahead. Bullets pelting like rain.

"Vick!"

Lucy called his name, the fear in her voice dragging things into focus.

The red button shone like a beacon, and he slammed his fist against it before darting to Frank.

In one swift motion, he lifted his limp body and staggered through the smoke and sweltering heat.

Collapsing on the lawn, he laid Frank on his back and searched for vital signs, finding a weak pulse.

A heavy raindrop fell on Frank's forehead.

Then another.

And another.

A siren wailed in the distance.

Help was coming.

It wasn't too late.

Not like last time.

CHAPTER 19

Lucy stood on the lawn in the downpour, watching the ambulance speed off with Frank and Beverly inside, on their way to the hospital in Primrose Valley.

She'd called Beverly as soon as she got off the phone with the 911 dispatcher. If it had been Vick trapped in a burning building, she'd want to know. She'd want to be by his side as soon as possible.

Thinking of Vick, she glanced over her shoulder. She'd lost sight of him in the commotion. The last place she remembered seeing him was in the backyard.

Her gut wrenched when she rounded the house and saw the smoldering remnants of the barn. The entire roof had caved in, and burnt timber and ash littered the ground. Thankfully, with the help of the storm, they'd been able to put the fire out quickly, before the entire building was engulfed in flames.

She found Vick sitting on the top step of the back porch, barely protected by the overhang. He was bent forward, shoulders hunched, gasping for air.

Panic gripped her chest. He'd inhaled too much smoke! She

should've made him ride in the ambulance with Frank. He needed to be checked out by a doctor.

She rushed over to him, trying not to sound as frantic as she felt. "Come on, you need to go to the hospital."

He didn't answer.

His eyes looked wild, and he fidgeted with his left hand, his fingers trembling.

It was even worse than she thought.

She sat beside him, fear creeping into her throat. "Vick, what's wrong?"

He continued to tap his fingers against his thumb, inhaling and exhaling in ragged breaths.

She grabbed his free hand, lacing her fingers through his, and pressed their palms together.

The contact seemed to snap him out of his trance.

He met her gaze, and her heart broke at the sorrow reflected in his eyes.

"Please, Vick. Tell me what's going on."

He glanced down at their entwined fingers, staring in silence.

Waiting with agonizing patience, Lucy prayed he'd respond.

~

Something about Lucy's touch soothed the tremor in Vick's hand.

He'd forgotten what it felt like to have someone who cared this deeply, a partner in life's most soul-wrenching moments.

Someone worthy of his trust.

Lucy was that person and so much more.

He drew in a breath—steadier this time—and met her gaze again, finding comfort in her eyes.

"I've never told anyone this before…" He hesitated, realizing he'd never even said the words out loud.

"I was diagnosed with PTSD." The detestable letters escaped

through clenched teeth and tasted bitter in his mouth. He hated the sound of the official diagnosis. Even inside his own head, he avoided calling it what it was. It made him feel weak.

"Oh, Vick. I'm so sorry." She squeezed his hand, fervent compassion etched into every feature.

He closed his eyes, still plagued by unbearable heat, choking on toxic fumes, as though caught in a merciless loop.

"We were on patrol in this run-down village surrounded by opium fields. Things seemed fairly routine until, out of nowhere, bullets rained down on us from every direction. I told my buddy Hodge to duck behind an SUV for cover."

His throat went dry, and he suddenly found it impossible to swallow.

You have to get through this....

He forced another breath, trying to block out the horrific memory.

"I swear I had no idea—" His voice cracked, and the panic rose in his chest, pressing against his rib cage until he nearly cried out in pain.

Lucy looped her arm through his, scooting closer as she offered support with her presence.

His breathing slowed.

"What happened?" she whispered, her eyes shimmering with tears.

"A car bomb." Guilt, remorse, and shame tumbled inside, overwhelming him with grief. "He never saw it coming. And it was my fault. If only I hadn't—"

"It's not your fault," she interrupted, gentle yet firm. "You couldn't have known. And you shouldn't live with that guilt. I don't think your friend would want you to."

He nodded, still wrestling with the bereavement and self-reproach.

Deep down, Vick knew Lucy was right. But on some level, the guilt helped him cope. He wanted to put the blame somewhere, and a random terrorist was too nebulous to carry the weight. There was so much about the war he still couldn't reconcile. He didn't know if he ever would.

Even as the thought churned in his mind, he knew Hodge's death alone wasn't what caused the PTSD. The news he got the next day had pushed him over the edge. But he wasn't sure how much more misery he could share in one sitting.

Leaning against him, Lucy rested her head on his shoulder, her silent tears sinking into his soaked shirt.

She didn't say another word, didn't offer any hollow platitudes or trite sayings. She merely clung to him, and her company said everything he needed.

"Thanks, Luce."

"For what?" She sniffled, tilting her chin to glimpse his face.

"For being here. For listening. For being someone I can trust. It's not easy to talk about my feelings. But you inspire me to put myself out there when it counts. I may not be vulnerable with everyone, but I want to be with you." He felt a sense of relief as he spoke, as though he should've said the words a long time ago.

He never thought he'd have this deep of a connection with anyone. And he never wanted to lose it.

"What do you say we head to the hospital and check on Frank?" he asked, wanting to make sure he was all right.

"I'd like that. But you're sure you're okay?"

He glanced at their hands again, perfectly molded together.

And for the first time in as long as he could remember, he could honestly say that he was.

~

Lucy gripped Vick's hand, anxiously awaiting an update as they sat in the hallway of Mountain Crest Hospital.

Her entire body ached from emotional exhaustion, especially her heart. She so badly wanted to take Vick's pain away, but she didn't know how. Helpless and out of her depth, all she could do was be there for him and pray it was enough.

Now, they restlessly waited for a verdict on Frank's condition.

Considering she'd visited this very hospital a few weeks ago, she couldn't wait to escape the harsh fluorescent lighting and pungent smell of sickness and cleaning chemicals. But she wouldn't dream of leaving until they knew Frank was all right.

Lucy thought about calling Cassie and the others, knowing they'd want to be here, too, but she decided to hold off until she could ask Beverly, in case she found it overwhelming.

As if on cue, Beverly emerged through the swinging door, her features pale yet calm. "He's going to be fine."

Tears of gratitude stung the backs of Lucy's eyes, and she sprang from the seat. "Praise God," she breathed, gathering Beverly in the kind of hug that said far more than words.

"Do they know what happened?" Vick asked, standing beside her.

"Like a stubborn fool, he decided to roast on his own." She dabbed her eyes with an embroidered handkerchief, her words softened by her intense relief. "He slipped on some spilled beans and dislocated his hip when he fell. He tried crawling to the machine to shut it off, but couldn't make it."

"I'm guessing it overheated, causing the fire, and Frank passed out in the smoke," Vick concluded.

Beverly nodded tearfully. "If you two hadn't arrived when you did, he might not be here today." She squeezed their hands, and Lucy breathed another silent thank-you that Vick had offered to go with her. She had no idea what she would've done if she'd been alone.

"I'd better get back to Frank. The doctor said he can have regular visitors tomorrow. I know he'd love to see you."

She hugged and thanked them both again before disappearing through the swinging door.

Lucy turned to Vick and smiled through her tears. "I'm so

glad he's going to be okay." All the energy seeped from her body along with her pent-up fear and anxiety.

He reached for her, and she leaned against him, relishing the weight of his arm around her.

"Hungry?" he asked.

Earlier, food had been the furthest thing from her mind, but now? "I'm famished," she admitted with a sheepish grin, regretting that their lunch from the diner had been ruined in the rain.

"Come on, let's change out of these wet clothes and get something to eat." With his arm still slung around her shoulders, they headed for the exit.

That's when she heard someone call her name, and her blood ran cold at the familiar voice.

CHAPTER 20

Every muscle in her body tensed, and Lucy tried to communicate with Dr. Dunlap telepathically.

Please don't say anything.... Please don't say anything....

While in the strictest sense, he honored doctor-patient confidentiality, as a small-town practitioner, he had a more casual approach, which she'd never minded... until now.

When they arrived at Mountain Crest, she'd been so focused on Frank, it never occurred to her that she might run into her own doctor, although he was known for regularly visiting patients throughout the hospital.

Now that he stood before her, she had no idea what to say. Or how to prevent a catastrophic mistake.

"H-hi, Dr. Dunlap," she stammered, casting a helpless glance at the exit sign.

So close to freedom, yet so very far away.

"Lucy." He repeated her name, sternly this time instead of surprised. "I've spoken to my colleague, and she tells me you haven't scheduled an appointment yet."

"I-I will. I've... been busy."

He frowned, although kindness and compassion shimmered

in his eyes. "This isn't something you should take lightly, Lucy. Please, don't delay any longer."

She nodded meekly, too terrified to look in Vick's direction.

Dr. Dunlap gave her a grandfatherly pat on the shoulder before bidding them good night and continuing his rounds.

Lucy stood rooted to the spot in agonizing regret. She'd meant to tell Vick about her condition eventually. But now, after everything he'd shared—his openness and vulnerability—and what he'd said about trusting her, guilt tore at her insides.

She'd kept something from him. Something important. And she hoped he'd understand.

"Luce..." He trailed off, as though afraid to finish his question.

When she finally met his gaze, her gut wrenched.

Confusion creased the edges of his eyes and mouth. She could tell he wanted to ask about the exchange, but wasn't sure how.

This wasn't how she'd planned on telling him, but what other option did she have?

"Not here," she murmured, anxious to flee the nauseating smell of ammonia and stale coffee.

Once they were settled inside the darkness of the Jeep, with the rain pelting the windshield, she felt more secure than under the bright, exposing lights of the hospital.

For simplicity, she asked him to take her straight home, and she'd have Jack drop her off at her car in the morning.

He nodded, his gaze fixed on the road.

For a few miles, Lucy couldn't find her voice. None of the words tumbling in her mind sounded right. No matter how she strung them together, they weren't enough.

"Luce," he said quietly. "Is everything okay?" His concern carried a twinge of cautious hesitation that stung her heart.

Did he sense she hadn't been completely forthcoming?

It's now or never. You have to tell him.

Wringing her hands in her lap, she confessed, "I saw Dr. Dunlap a few weeks ago about my migraines."

"*Migraines?*" Vick asked, accentuating the plurality.

Lucy winced, immediately aware of how bad it sounded.

There was no getting around the fact that she'd purposefully misled him. And although she'd had a good reason, she wasn't sure that would matter anymore. Fear rippled through her.

Blinking back tears, she continued. "The migraine at the Pumpkin & Paws event wasn't my first."

She noticed his grip tighten on the steering wheel, but he didn't make a sound.

"I didn't tell you because I didn't want you to worry until I had more answers. And honestly, I'm still processing it all myself."

Her rationale had made so much sense at the time; it not only seemed reasonable, but kind.

Now, she swallowed the lump of shame clinging to her throat like a boil.

How had she let this happen?

She braved another glance at Vick.

He clamped his teeth together, a barricade against the accusations she rightfully deserved.

It was time she told him everything. No holding back.

"Dr. Dunlap referred me to a specialist in LA for an MRI. But I haven't made the appointment yet. That's what he meant when he said I shouldn't delay. They primarily want to rule out... a tumor." She could barely manage to say the word, although it had been lurking in the back of her mind for weeks.

In the dim light from the dash, she could see the veins pop on the back of his hand as his knuckles clenched.

She waited in tortured silence for him to say something —anything.

Finally, he whispered, "It might be cancer?" in a voice so raspy and strained, she ached to reach out to him.

But she kept her hands in her lap, coiled around the damp fabric of her peacoat. "It's a possibility." The admission tasted toxic on the tip of her tongue, and she scoured her internal well of positivity for a salve, but no odes of optimism came to mind.

Only cold fear, clawing its way to the surface.

He reached for her hand in the darkness, and Lucy nearly wept at his touch.

But it ended all too briefly, as though he'd acted on impulse, then thought better of it.

Both hands back on the steering wheel, he asked, "Why didn't you tell me?" His audible hurt and confusion heaped onto her regret.

Oh, how she wished she could go back in time and make a different choice.

"I haven't told anyone. I've been processing, trying to figure out what I want to do."

"I don't get it. What's there to decide? You get the MRI. You take every test you need to take. Then you take every treatment necessary to fight whatever it is. You face it head-on, surrounded by the people who care about you. You don't keep them out." His tone was desperate, almost pleading.

"It's not that simple." Tears scalded her eyes, and she blinked rapidly, fighting to stave them off. How could she possibly explain what she was going through? Or why she wanted to cling to the thin thread of hope for as long as possible? She knew her reasoning sounded foolish. Possibly even dangerous. But she couldn't let go. She couldn't stop pretending.

Holding her breath, she stole another sideways glance, pained to see his tense, tormented expression. Clearly, he hadn't liked her answer. While she fully understood his hurt and apprehension, she couldn't read his intense reaction. And it worried her.

Vick parked close to her cabin, the headlights illuminating the short trek to the front door.

Lucy sensed it was her cue to leave, but she couldn't move. She couldn't walk away with so many things left unsaid, with the awful tension between them.

Raindrops tapped against the windshield, accentuating the suffocating silence.

Vick jumped out of the Jeep and strode around to the passenger side to open the door for her, his gray eyes dark and murky.

Unsure what to say, she hopped down, her boots sinking into the mud.

He slammed the door behind her.

Droplets clung to her hair and slipped down her collar, but she didn't care. She couldn't see anything beyond the searing pain in Vick's gaze.

"Please, talk to me," she pleaded, desperate to fix her mistake. "Tell me why you're so upset."

"I can't." His words escaped through gritted teeth, and he stared at her with visceral anguish.

"Why?"

"Because I don't know what to say." Frustration seeped from his voice, and he ran his fingers through his sopping-wet hair. "I wish you weren't going through this. I wish you trusted me enough to let me in. When you love someone, you invite them into the good and the bad."

For a moment, everything else faded away. Had Vick said he loved her? A part of her wanted to pause and soak it in, but she needed to hear the rest, to understand his wound and repair the damage she'd caused.

"You don't shut them out. You don't hide things from them. You don't go through it all on your own." His eyes glinted with grief, and rain poured down his face, revealing a soft vulnerability normally hidden behind his strong, stoic features. "You don't die and deprive them of the chance to say goodbye—"

"Vick." Finally understanding what it was really about, she stepped toward him, wrapping her arms around his shoulders.

With a deep shudder, he leaned into her embrace, and for several seconds, she simply held him.

After a moment, he murmured, "My mom had ovarian cancer during my second deployment and didn't tell me. The day after my buddy Hodge died in the bombing, I got the phone call that she was gone. I never even knew she'd been sick."

Her heart breaking, she hugged him tighter. "I'm so, so sorry." Tears mingled with rainwater, cascading down her cheeks.

"The panic attacks started after that. I couldn't keep it together. And I lost everything that ever mattered to me."

"That's not going to happen this time." She tilted her chin and met his gaze.

"I don't think I can do this, Lucy."

Her pulse raced, unsure what he meant.

He moved to pull away, and before she knew what she was doing, she cupped the side of his face, drawing his mouth to hers.

~

Every fiber in Vick's being ignited the instant Lucy kissed him, filling him with a hungry desperation.

He needed her more than anything he'd ever needed in his life.

And yet, his heart ached with an unbearable pain. The kind of pain he swore to avoid, no matter the cost.

As though against his will, his arms encircled her waist, drawing her against him. To feel, if only for a moment, the sensation of being bonded beyond time and space.

For once, he'd been close to having the unattainable—a connection that transcended all the trauma he'd experienced.

He'd had hope.

All those nights lying awake, dreaming about Lucy's elusive kiss, he wondered what it would be like to finally capture it. He never imagined it would taste so bittersweet, that it would lift him high above the clouds, only to smash him back down to earth.

Unbidden, his thoughts flew to one of the most quoted lines from *Peter Pan and Wendy*.

"Dreams do come true, if only we wish hard enough."

A nice sentiment, but people always forgot the second line.

"You can have anything in life if you will sacrifice everything else for it."

But once you do, there's no going back.

Lucy's fingers wound through his damp hair, sending currents of heat coursing through his body.

Everything about being with Lucy, right here and now, felt right.

But she'd lied to him. Or at least, kept him from the truth.

Just like his mother had.

The moment he simultaneously found out about her illness and death was the moment he'd lost any sense of well-being and rightness in the world.

He'd learned that everything good in life could be gone in an instant. And in most cases, you never saw it coming. You couldn't prepare. You couldn't brace yourself. The agony hit like a tsunami, dragging you down until you could no longer breathe. Until your limbs could no longer kick and grasp for help. Until you slipped away into oblivion, which is how he'd been going through each day—not dead, not fully alive.

Then he'd met Lucy.

She made him question everything, made him yearn for more.

Against his better judgment, he lost himself in the kiss that unlocked thoughts he'd wrestled with for so long. But on the heels of his newfound clarity, a darker revelation gnashed its teeth, reminding him he'd been wrong to hope. Wrong to think he could change.

He could cope and survive, nothing more.

Summoning all his restraint, he broke away, holding her at arm's length.

She gazed up at him, droplets collecting on her lashes, dripping from her hair.

Even now, he'd never seen anything more beautiful, more radiant and vibrant. But like Neverland, what they had wasn't real. It couldn't last. He needed to grow up. The harshness of life had a way of stealing everything good when you least expected it. And it was better to let go before it was ripped away.

"I can't do this." He stepped back, dropping his hands.

"Vick—"

"I'm sorry. I just can't." He strode toward the Jeep, unsure how he summoned the ability to walk away from her.

It felt like his heart had been torn from his chest and remained where she stood.

But it was better that way.

Faced with the alternative, he preferred being numb.

CHAPTER 21

Covering her face with a pillow, Lucy shielded her eyes from the offending sunlight. Her temples throbbed, but not from a migraine this time. She'd sobbed uncontrollably all night, unable to wrap her head around what had happened.

Sick with grief that she'd caused Vick so much pain—unintentional or not—she longed to go back in time and do things differently. But her only option was to move forward.

And for once, her unwavering optimism faltered. Would Vick ever forgive her?

Her fingertips floated to her lips, tracing the outline of their kiss.

She'd never been kissed like that before—fiercely passionate and tender all at once. So life-giving yet destructive, especially the moment he walked away.

Tears pricked her eyes, and an oppressive hollowness settled in her chest. The new normal. How could life without Vick ever be joyful again?

Peeling back the covers, she inched out of bed in slow, unmotivated movements to get ready for the day.

The day...

A pitiful groan escaped her lips when she realized the significance of the date.

The Library Benefit Banquet was being held at the inn that evening.

And they were supposed to go together.

Her gaze fluttered to the costume hanging on the exterior of the antique wardrobe. She gingerly caressed the pale-blue fabric of the dress, another sob catching in her throat.

How could she go by herself? She couldn't bear the thought, let alone actually go through with it.

But she couldn't let Jack and Kat down, either. This event was the most important one out of all the fall festivities they'd filmed so far. She needed to make a video for her channel, even if she had to do it on her own.

Her chest squeezed again, leaving her breathless. Maybe she should tell Jack what happened? He must've noticed whatever was going on between her and Vick.

A thought pushed its way to the forefront of her mind.

She *did* need to talk to Jack.

About her migraines.

Vick's pointed accusations had plagued her all night.

When you love someone, you invite them into the good and the bad. You don't shut them out.

Would her family be hurt that she hadn't told them? And what about her friends? What about Sadie? They'd been through so much together.

Vick reminded her that she had something special—a supportive and loving community.

In hindsight, she regretted shutting them out.

Maybe it was time to rectify her mistake.

She found her brother exactly where she expected—sipping coffee in one of the Adirondack chairs by the lake, Fitz by his side, watching the sun shimmer across the surface of the water, slowly waking the snow-capped mountains in the distance.

Her brother often came out to this spot first thing in the morning, and she had a standing invitation to join him, but she rarely woke up before seven.

She drew closer, leaves crunching beneath her boots.

Jack glanced over his shoulder, a startled glint in his eyes. When he spotted her, his features relaxed. "You're up early."

"Mind if I join you?" Without waiting for an answer, she sat in the chair beside him, and he handed her his Coleman thermos.

She unscrewed the cap, using it as a cup, and poured herself some rich, aromatic coffee. "Incredible view."

Mist lifted off the water, wafting into the clear blue sky. Everything sparkled after the rain, basking in the luminous glow of a fresh start.

But her brother wasn't looking at the view. He stared at something small and circular in his hand.

Lucy gasped. "Is that—"

Jack held it up for her to see. The stunning pearl-and-emerald ring glistened in the light.

"May I?" Mesmerized, she held out her hand and Jack placed it in her palm.

Up close, she noticed the delicate engravings in the yellow gold that resembled slender leaves. Her throat tightened. While it looked vintage, she suspected her brother had it custom made. The intricate, elegant design bore an uncanny resemblance to mistletoe. Knowing the significance, she could barely contain her emotion.

"Do you think she'll like it?" Jack's voice carried an uncommon tremor of hesitation.

"She's going to love it." Lucy blinked back tears, wrestling with both unbelievable joy and hidden sorrow. She couldn't be happier for her brother, but the contrast to her own shattered love life was difficult to ignore.

"You know," he said softly as she handed back the ring, "there was a time I didn't think this would ever happen for me. Or if I even wanted it to."

Lucy recalled how heartbroken Jack had been when his high school girlfriend left him after graduation, knowing full well he'd been preparing to start a life together.

"After everything you've been through, what made you want to give it another try?"

"It's hard to explain, but meeting Kat made me realize what I'd experienced the first time around was infatuation. I'd built up a picture in my mind that wasn't real. But when you find the right person, it's like looking into a mirror. They show you the best and worst parts of yourself, which helps you grow beyond what you could achieve on your own. We're partners, in the truest sense of the word. In business and in life." He gave a wry grin. "And it doesn't hurt that she's easy on the eyes, makes me laugh, and can cook a mean stack of flapjacks."

Lucy smiled through her tears, her heart near bursting. "I couldn't be more excited for you two. When are you proposing?"

"I'm still working on it. But you'll be the first to know." He slipped the ring into the wooden box and closed the lid. "But that's not what you came out here to talk to me about. What's on your mind?"

Lucy squirmed, not wanting to follow up his good news with her health problems. "Oh, it's nothing that can't wait. I'll tell you later."

"We're here now. Spill it."

"I don't want to ruin the mood."

"Okay, now you have to tell me." He set down his coffee mug and shifted in the chair to face her.

Clearly, he wasn't going to take no for an answer.

Lucy gathered a breath, grappling for the right words. "I saw Dr. Dunlap a few weeks ago."

"Oh, yeah? What for?"

She could tell he was moderating his reaction, not wanting to jump to conclusions.

"I've been having migraines off and on for a while now. I thought he could help me figure out why they're happening."

"And did he?" Tension crept into his voice.

For his sake, she kept her tone even and calm, though her pulse raced out of control. She curled her fingers in her lap to stop the trembling. "Unfortunately, no. He wants me to make an appointment with a specialist."

"When?"

"As soon as possible."

He frowned, doing the mental math. "Wait. You said you saw Dr. Dunlap a few weeks ago?"

She nodded, knowing where his question was headed.

"And you haven't made the appointment yet?" His expression was stern with a large dose of loving concern.

"I will. I promise."

"Today?"

"If you're going to twist my arm about it." She attempted a lighthearted inflection, hoping to add some levity.

"Whatever it takes. If I have to, I'll sic Kat and her Krav Maga moves on you," he teased, then quickly grew serious. "Let me know when it is because I'm coming with you."

A small smile cracked her somber exterior. That was so like Jack. The consummate big brother, always looking out for her. "It's in LA. I'll be gone the whole day."

"I don't care about that. I want to be there."

"Fine, but only because I don't want Kat to put me in a choke hold."

They shared a laugh, and once again Lucy wished she'd asked for this kind of support a long time ago.

If only she could find a way to fix things with Vick, she'd tell him he'd been right. And thank him for helping her see what she truly needed.

"Have you told Mom and Dad?" Jack's question interrupted her thoughts, presenting a new problem.

While she wanted to be forthcoming, her mother could be… a lot. And she wasn't sure how she'd react to the news.

"Not yet, but I will," she promised, adding, "Honestly, Jack. I know it could be something serious, but it's probably nothing. It might be something as simple as a gluten intolerance." She wasn't sure who she needed to convince more, her brother or herself.

"Well, let's pray you're allergic to wheatgrass and bean sprouts instead."

"Good idea." She grinned, feeling a thousand times better.

As they continued to talk, Lucy realized she didn't have to decide between facing reality and choosing optimism.

She could still cling to hope.

When it came to her health.

And with Vick.

~

Vick shoved the wad of T-shirts into an oversize duffel bag, wrestling with an ever-persistent voice of doubt. It began as a whisper, barely audible in the back of his mind, second-guessing his decision to skip town. But the more stuff he packed, the louder the voice grew, determined to talk him out of it.

That's when he started rationalizing.

Leaving during the Library Benefit Banquet had been the arrangement all along. It made the most sense, like ripping off a Band-Aid with your eyes closed.

There was only one reason he'd put the plan on pause.

Lucy.

Hard as he tried, he couldn't stop thinking about her, replaying every agonizing second from last night.

He hadn't just been a hypocrite. He'd been a coward.

The thought of losing Lucy to her illness terrified him more than anything he'd faced before. And yet, he'd walked away when she needed him most.

The realization made his throat and chest burn like he'd downed a shot of acid.

He glanced at the dresser. His costume for the evening lay folded on top.

Part of him wanted to pull it on and go to Lucy right now, to plead for her forgiveness. In the harsh light of a new day, he knew he'd reacted too strongly. He'd been focused on himself when he should've tried to see the situation from her perspective.

Whether she admitted it or not, his gut told him that she was scared. And keeping her health concerns a secret had been her coping mechanism.

Instead of lashing out because of his own internal issues, he should've been there for her.

Even faced with this knowledge, he wasn't sure he could be the man she deserved—the man she needed. The one time he'd witnessed her migraine, he almost had a full-blown panic attack. He barely got through it. What if it happened again and he couldn't keep his own symptoms in check?

Or was that simply an excuse because he didn't know if he'd survive losing someone else he loved?

He honestly wasn't sure.

Emotionally defeated, he reached for the next item to toss in the bag.

Frank's book.

He held the heavy hardback in his hand, feeling the weight of it against his palm.

Frank's doctor wanted to keep him in the hospital one more day for observation, which presented Vick with a complicated choice.

With one last glance at the glossy cover, he stuffed it inside the duffel, his decision made.

CHAPTER 22

His back rigid, Vick sat beside Frank's hospital bed, questioning his decision to come. He wasn't the hospital-visit type. He didn't invest in people. He didn't get attached.

He'd kept to himself most of his adult life and old habits die hard.

Death...

That's exactly what this place brought to mind.

The chemical smells, beeping of heart monitors, the general aura of sickness and suffering, every detail served as a reminder of the fragility of life.

And when someone died, they left their loved ones behind to pick up the pieces, to pretend to move on, all while knowing it's an impossible task.

"I'm going to the cafeteria for a cup of tea." Beverly bent down and kissed Frank's cheek, a subtle gesture that spoke volumes. "Can I get anyone anything?"

Both men declined, and Vick noticed Frank's gaze remained on his wife until she left the room.

"She's something else, isn't she?" Frank's typical gruff tone thawed, revealing his affection. "Tonight is her big night, you know. The library shindig at the inn. I told her she could go without me, but she wouldn't hear it."

She was brave and selfless, Vick noted. All things he wasn't.

Frank shifted his gaze from the doorway, resting it on Vick. "I'm not one for flowery thank yous," he grunted.

"And I'm not one for accepting them."

"Then you'll settle for a handshake?"

"Yes, sir."

As they shook hands, Frank stared at the eagle tattoo on Vick's forearm. "From the Marines?"

Vick retracted his hand and yanked down his sleeve. "I got it before I enlisted."

"Sentimental reasons?"

"Something like that."

Frank tugged on the collar of his hospital gown, revealing a tattoo of a bird on his shoulder. "It's a nightingale. Any guesses why I got it?"

"A woman?"

"You're pretty sharp." Frank smiled to offset his sarcastic quip. "It's always a woman. Either your girl or your mother. Which is yours?"

Vick shifted on the uncomfortable plastic chair, not meeting Frank's gaze. "My mom. It's her favorite Bible verse. *Was* her favorite," he corrected.

"Let me guess. It goes a little something like, 'Those who hope in the Lord will renew their strength. They will soar on wings like eagles; they will run and not grow weary, they will walk and not be faint.'"

"That's the one," Vick said bitterly. "Lot of good it did her."

"What do you mean?"

"She had cancer, which means the last leg of her life she wasn't anything *but* weary and faint. And then she died. So much for soaring on wings like an eagle." He flexed his forearm, not for the first time regretting his choice in ink.

"Who says she isn't?"

Vick balked. Sure, Frank was older, but had he completely lost his hearing?

"She *died*," he repeated for emphasis, even though the word still tasted acrid on his tongue.

"I'm familiar with the term. And I'm sorry for your loss, son. But just because a person leaves this earth, doesn't mean their hope was in vain. Trust me. I've been giving death a lot of thought these days." He lifted his wrist, showing off his IV. "I bet your mom's in Heaven right now, giving her wings a good spin around the Pearly Gates."

To his surprise, the corner of Vick's mouth crept upward in an involuntary smile. He welcomed the image.

"When I go," Frank continued, "I like to think I'll still roast coffee in Heaven. No decaf, purely the good stuff. And if I get distracted, I won't burn the place down." He chuckled, then softened. "The lie isn't in hoping, son. It's in thinking we can live this life on our own. Take it from someone who's tried."

Vick leaned forward, scooting to the edge of the seat. "Do you ever miss your old life? When you were on your own?"

Frank's eyebrows knit together as he pondered the question. "It was difficult at first, learning to share my space, realizing my actions impacted the people around me. But even when it's hard, it's worth it for all that I've gained. Especially Bevy. I'd give up coffee for that woman."

Vick expected Frank to chuckle again, but he didn't. Instead, he peered at him with a penetrating stare.

"Did you ever figure out if you're running toward or away from something?"

"Neither," Vick said quickly and with conviction, as if his heart responded before his mind had time to think.

At some point during their conversation, he'd come to a decision without even realizing it—one his soul had known all along.

He met Frank's gaze. "I'm not going anywhere."

The older man smiled, satisfied with Vick's response. "Then I have a proposition for you."

~

Fingers shaking with nervous energy, Lucy swept her blond curls into a low ponytail and handed Sadie the blue satin ribbon. "Can you tie this for me?"

"Of course." Sadie fussed with the bow until she achieved the perfect shape, then whispered, "How are you feeling?"

"Same as five minutes ago," Lucy teased. She'd told Sadie about her migraines earlier that afternoon, and her friend's concern was sweet, if not a little too persistent. To her credit, she'd reacted better than Lucy's parents when she'd called them shortly afterward. Her mother had fussed relentlessly, armed with even more incentive to pressure Lucy's return home, while her father vowed to hire the best doctors money could buy. It had taken her almost an hour to convince them she had things under control.

Although she hadn't had a migraine in several days, Lucy had called the clinic and made an appointment. Since she'd put it off for so long, they'd squeezed her in the next day, late in the afternoon. Finally having a date and time set in stone filled her with a strange mix of relief and apprehension.

"What do you think? Is it too much?" Jayla emerged from the bathroom of the Zephyr Suite in a silvery ball gown that contrasted beautifully with her skin tone.

"Not at all!" Lucy assured her, beaming with delight. "You look gorgeous."

"Are you sure? I'm starting to think I should have chosen

something more subtle than Cinderella. Maybe from a contemporary novel so I could wear my own clothes."

"You were made for this dress. Come sit. I have the finishing touch." Lucy rose from the small vanity table and gave Jayla her seat, grateful they'd decided to get ready with her, in case she backed out at the last minute.

Plus, she needed the distraction. She'd given a note to Bill earlier and asked him to hand-deliver it to Vick. If he showed up tonight, she'd know he'd forgiven her, and they could work on moving forward.

If he didn't...

She involuntarily shuddered.

"What else do you think the outfit needs?" Jayla asked, gazing at her reflection in the mirror. She'd wound her thick black hair into an elegant bun on top of her head, which called attention to the blue velvet choker accentuating her long, graceful neck.

Smiling, Lucy lifted the vintage tiara from her bag, the one Penny helped her find, and carefully set it in place. "There. Now your transformation is complete."

"Wow," Jayla breathed, lightly grazing the glittering gemstones.

"You look amazing." Sadie stood behind her in the mirror, and Lucy nearly laughed out loud at the startling contrast between their costumes.

Sadie had also gone with a fairy-tale theme, but rather than a princess, she'd chosen the wicked witch from *Hansel and Gretel,* complete with a prosthetic nose.

It was so like Sadie, when everyone else wanted to look beautiful, she went for the element of surprise.

Jayla giggled, pointing to Sadie's bulbous beak. "Your wart is falling off."

"Not again," Sadie sighed, jabbing it with her finger. "Where's the glue?"

"Here." Jayla grabbed the bottle off the vanity. "I'll help you."

While they fixed Sadie's wart, Lucy slipped out to see if Kat and Hana needed any last-minute help.

At least, that's the excuse she gave.

Secretly, she couldn't wait a second longer to see if Vick had arrived.

Halfway down the winding staircase, her breath caught in her throat.

She gripped the banister until her knuckles blanched, afraid she might fall thanks to the sudden surge of emotion.

He had his back to her, but she'd recognize the green tights and feathered hat anywhere.

She knew he'd come!

As though transported by pixie dust, she floated down the remaining steps, pausing at the bottom.

Any moment now, her heart would burst with happiness.

"You came." The warble in her voice betrayed her, but she didn't care.

It took all of her self-control not to rush into his arms.

Her Peter Pan turned, a smile on his face.

But it wasn't the one she expected.

CHAPTER 23

Vick shoved the Jeep into park and jumped out of the driver's seat, adrenaline pumping through his body.

He'd already planned to show up tonight to fight for a second chance, but the moment he read Lucy's message, his tentative hope skyrocketed far beyond his wildest expectations.

It had been a simple note, on a simple slip of paper.

A quote from their favorite book.

"Never say goodbye because goodbye means going away and going away means forgetting."

His entire body ached to hold her, to kiss her again, to assure her he wouldn't be going anywhere. And he didn't care if the whole town witnessed it.

Earnest anticipation spurred each step as he passed beneath the wisteria-covered pergola on the side of the inn, heading toward the music and festive commotion.

Stopping at the perimeter of the party, he searched the collage of faces.

People laughed and mingled over fancy hors d'oeuvres, all clad in creative, elaborate costumes.

Sparkling string lights and dazzling candlelit chandeliers illuminated the expansive backyard, which had a dance floor on one side and long banquet tables arranged on the other. Books and flowers were used as decorations in equal measure, and although Vick wasn't one for pomp and circumstance, even he was impressed.

He continued searching the crowd, his pulse keeping time with the upbeat melody of the live band, until his gaze finally locked on Lucy.

Mid-inhale, his lungs stopped working.

Dressed in a blue satiny dress that enhanced the color of her eyes, she stole the show as Wendy Moira Angela Darling—the perfect match to his Peter Pan.

For a beat, all he could do was stare and soak up her beauty.

She chatted with a guest from the inn—Jayla, if he remembered correctly.

Eager to capture her attention, he strode toward them, stopping short when a man appeared by her side.

A man he'd never seen before... dressed as Peter Pan.

The stranger handed her a glass of champagne, and Vick flinched when their fingers grazed.

He waited for the intruder to walk away, wanting to write off the exchange as a fluke. But the man didn't budge. Even worse, he stood much closer to Lucy than necessary.

She smiled, inviting the man into their conversation.

His gut twisting, Vick backed away, ducking around the side of the house. Hidden from view, he gathered a stabilizing breath, bracing himself against the brick exterior as he tried to register what he'd seen.

Had she come with someone else? And if so, what about the note she'd left? Had he completely misunderstood the meaning?

Confused and conflicted, he paced in the darkness, sorting through his agitated thoughts.

A few days ago, he might have read the situation as a sign to retreat.

But now, after countless hours of wrestling with his emotions, coming to grips with his past, giving up wasn't an option.

He needed to tell Lucy how he felt and face whatever humiliation and heartache might follow.

He stepped out of the shadows, colliding with another man's chest.

The man grunted an apology, and Vick met Rhett's panicked gaze.

"Sorry. I didn't see you." Sweat beaded Rhett's forehead as he tossed a frantic glance over his shoulder.

Vick followed his gaze and spotted a petite brunette in the crowd dressed in plain clothes.

Momentarily distracted from his own plight, he asked, "What's going on?"

Without a response, Rhett ducked down the side of the building, and Vick followed, alarm bells ringing in his head.

Something wasn't right.

"Who is that woman? The one you keep avoiding." He closely observed Rhett's expression in the dim light.

"I didn't think she'd be here tonight." His motions were twitchy and agitated.

"Who? Your ex?" Vick hazarded a guess.

Was Rhett being hounded for alimony payments or child support? He didn't seem like the kind of guy to shirk his responsibilities.

Rhett ran his fingers through his sandy hair, misery etched into every fine line and wrinkle. "I don't know how much time I have left, so I'd better just tell you."

"Tell me what?" Vick pressed, not liking Rhett's tone or choice in phrasing. What did he mean by how much time he had left?

"She's not an ex," Rhett confessed with a labored sigh. "She's my parole officer."

~

In the midst of their small talk, Lucy searched the crowd, looking for Vick.

Why wasn't he here yet? Dinner would be starting soon, then dancing. She didn't want to miss a single moment of tonight with him.

Kat, with the help of the planning committee, had transformed the entire backyard into a book-lover's utopia, complete with a six-tier cake designed to resemble spiral bookcases. And the literary-inspired fare didn't stop there. Guests could also sip Butterbeer from *Harry Potter* while nibbling on Caraway Seed Cake from *Jane Eyre*, among many other edible, bookish delights.

But Lucy didn't want to touch a single crumb until Vick arrived.

She cast a sideways glance at Brennan Hollingsworth—her mother's favorite bachelor and object of her relentless matchmaking attempts—who'd just said something to make Jayla laugh.

She still couldn't believe her mother had done this to her. Or could she? Elaine Gardener wasn't above chicanery. Brennan admitted Elaine had called him and suggested he make a surprise appearance. Of course, her mother knew her favorite fictional character, so his costume was purposefully chosen to win her favor.

Sneaky, to say the least.

Luckily, Brennan seemed to be hitting it off with Jayla, so once Vick arrived, she wouldn't be responsible for keeping him company. Based on their easy chemistry, she didn't think Jayla would mind stepping in. So far, the two had a remarkable amount in common.

"So, Jayla, what do you do?" Brennan asked.

"I'm an American Sign Language instructor and interpreter."

"She works primarily with women and children in shelters where the need is often unmet," Lucy added, knowing Jayla was too modest to mention that part on her own.

Brennan made a motion with his hands, and Jayla smiled.

"Was that sign language?" Lucy asked, admittedly surprised.

Jayla nodded. "He said he was impressed."

Lucy couldn't help noticing that Jayla looked rather impressed herself.

"My roommate in college lost his hearing as a child," Brennan explained. "So I picked up some sign language to better communicate with him. I also learned a lot about what life is like for the deaf and hard of hearing. Sadly, in a lot of ways, he was overlooked or ignored."

"That's why I love what I do," Jayla said with infectious passion. "So many people don't have a voice. And if I can help with that in some small way, I consider myself blessed." Something in her expression shifted as she added, "But it isn't always easy. Sometimes, it feels like fighting an uphill battle. Our country has come a long way, but, in my opinion, there still isn't enough awareness. And it's hard to get the word out."

"That's true." Brennan gave a sober nod and shared an experience with his roommate that opened his eyes to some of the issues.

While they bonded, Lucy listened, intently at first, but she increasingly found it hard to concentrate. Time continued to pass, but Vick still hadn't shown.

Why wasn't he here yet?

She refused to believe he simply wasn't coming. There had to be another explanation, a reason for the delay.

For the hundredth time, she stole a glance at her phone, but no new calls or texts had come through.

Should she call him?

She pulled up his number, debating her next move, then set her phone facedown on the bistro table.

No need to panic. He'd show. She was certain.

"Excuse me?" A petite brunette in a black blazer approached. "Have you been taking photos of the event all night?"

"Off and on, yes."

"May I take a look at them?"

She didn't offer an explanation, but Lucy was too preoccupied to question her. Careful not to catch her hair in the strap, she slipped the camera from around her neck and placed it in the woman's outstretched hand.

"Are you looking for something in particular?" Lucy didn't recognize the woman and couldn't figure out which literary character she was supposed to be.

"I'm looking for someone I thought would be here tonight."

You and me both, she muttered internally. "Who are you looking for? Maybe I've seen them."

The woman didn't respond, her attention focused on the LCD monitor as she scrolled through the recent photos. "Aha! I knew it." Mission accomplished, she handed the camera back to Lucy. "Thanks for your time." Without another word, she headed toward the inn.

Strange.

Lucy glanced at the candid photograph on the small, rectangular screen.

It was a snapshot of her brother talking to Rhett Douglas.

CHAPTER 24

For several seconds, Vick stood motionless, trying to gauge if he'd heard Rhett correctly, almost certain he hadn't. "I don't understand. What do you mean she's your parole officer?"

"Just what it sounds like. Being in Poppy Creek is a violation of my parole. I've seen her around town looking for me, but I've tried to lay low."

A thousand questions swirled in Vick's mind, and he blurted the first one that jumped out. "If she's looking for you, why didn't she just ask someone where you live or work?"

"They usually don't ask because questioning the wrong person could tip off the parolee, giving them time to run. They prefer to do reconnaissance on their own to keep the element of surprise. I don't think she's aware that I know she's here."

Rhett spoke with the casual, first-hand knowledge of a confirmed offender, but Vick still found it hard to believe. The man didn't seem like a criminal.

"If what you're saying is true, then what were you in for?"

Rhett dropped his gaze to the ground. "Armed robbery. Third

strike. I got twenty-five to life, but thanks to a prison chaplain who became my advocate, I got an early release."

"Armed robbery?" Vick frowned, unable to wrap his head around the information.

"My gun was fake, but my buddy's wasn't. According to the jury, it didn't matter. We were served the same sentence."

Vick paced in the shadows, both hands clasped behind his head, which had started to hum. None of this sounded right. "Does Jack know?"

"Yeah, he knows." Rhett's voice strained with emotion, becoming gravelly. "Jack said he believes in giving people a second chance, especially when they're hard to come by."

Vick stopped pacing. That sounded like Jack alright. And he couldn't say he disagreed, but something still didn't make sense. "If you know she's looking for you, why haven't you left town yet? And why break parole in the first place?"

Rhett cleared his throat, his eyes glinting in the moonlight as it filtered through the lattice. "Because I came to Poppy Creek to do something, and I won't leave until I have."

"What'd you come to do?"

"I came to meet my son. And tell him I'm sorry."

Rhett's words collided in Vick's mind, shifting and locking together as the pieces fell into place.

But even as the picture formed, Vick refused to see it.

He took a step backward, wanting the conversation to end.

But Rhett had already gone too far, said too much.

"I was young," he said slowly, as though beginning a morbid bedtime story. "I was already working two jobs, and so was my wife, but we were barely able to make ends meet. Then, we got pregnant, and I knew she wouldn't be able to work the same hours, if at all. I didn't know how we were going to survive." He drew in a pained breath, as though his chest physically ached. "I confided in a buddy of mine, who said we could make some quick money by knocking off ATMs. I knew it was wrong, but I was desperate. Which isn't an excuse. If I could go back in time, I would. That one decision cost me everything."

Even now, he sounded desperate, desperate to be believed, maybe even understood.

But the barricade around Vick's heart didn't budge. He barely wanted to listen, let alone sympathize.

And yet, he couldn't bring himself to walk away.

Rhett took the opening.

"The first two times were ATMs, then my buddy got a tip on a bank that would be an easy job. One last hit, then we'd be set. We'd never have to do another job again." The words dripped with scorn, as if, looking back, Rhett couldn't believe he'd fallen for it. "He said we should carry plastic guns, in case we ran into any trouble and needed to improvise. Of course, he assured me we wouldn't. It wasn't until he shot a security guard that I realized his gun wasn't fake."

Rhett's face twisted, visibly tormented by what they'd done. "When things went south, my buddy bolted, but I stayed behind to apply pressure to the bullet wound, knowing I'd be caught. Fortunately, the guard didn't lose too much blood, and eventually pulled through. They caught the other guy two days later, preparing to flee to Mexico."

The details sounded like a bad *True Crimes* episode, and Vick wrestled with conflicting emotions, both abhorrence and then unwanted admiration when Rhett shared how he'd given up his chance to escape.

In the end, Vick settled on detachment and denial.

Good for Rhett for paying his dues, but the sordid tale had nothing to do with him.

"Robbing that first ATM was a life-altering decision. I lost my wife and my child. And when I got out, I learned she'd died years earlier, and I had no idea where to find my son. It took me three years to track him down. And when I did, I was too afraid to tell him who I was, in case I lost him again." Rhett took a timid step toward him.

Vick instinctively stepped back, and Rhett winced, but he didn't look surprised.

"I should've told you that you're my son. And I'm sorry for stealing time with you without being forthcoming. I don't blame you for being angry or not wanting anything to do with me." His voice crackled, and in the murky shadows, his eyes gleamed, damp with tears. "What I did was wrong. And I'm sorry. I know it ruined far more lives than my own. And I wish I could take it back. But I never stopped loving you or your mother, although I understand her decision."

Vick's throat burned, and his ears rang with each word Rhett spoke.

Rhett… his father… he still couldn't reconcile the two.

What was he supposed to say? How was he supposed to feel?

"I don't know how much time I have left, but if you want to talk, I live off Old Highway, down by the river. I'm the only one there, so you can't miss me."

Vick stared blankly, unable to speak.

Unable to process anything.

His entire world had flipped inside out.

What was he supposed to do now?

~

Lucy left the party in a despondent daze.

Vick hadn't come.

Maybe it was naive to think her simple note would have fixed everything. Maybe what they'd shared simply wasn't enough.

As reality sank in, her heart crumpled inside her chest.

She stepped into the stillness of the parking lot, relishing the cold air against her face and neck. Most of the guests were still mingling in the backyard, not wanting the magical evening to end. But she looked forward to finally being alone to sit in her sadness. Putting on a brave, jovial face all night had left her empty and exhausted.

"Lucy!"

Surprised by the sound of her name, Lucy spun around.

Morgan Withers sashayed down the front steps of the inn, clad in a glitzy flapper gown as Daisy Buchanan from *The Great Gatsby*. Her spindly heels teetered in the gravel as she crossed the driveway toward Lucy. "I'm so glad I caught you before you left."

"Hi, Morgan. Is there something I can do for you?" Lucy summoned a smile, although she really just wanted to go home.

"In a manner of speaking, yes." Her immaculately made-up features settled into a strange, self-important smirk. "I've been watching you closely the last several days."

Lucy didn't think it would be polite to mention that she'd noticed—and found it unsettling—so she simply responded, "Oh?"

"I first stumbled on your YouTube channel a few weeks ago. I knew right away you had a special *it* factor, attractive yet approachable. That's hard to find. You're the kind of girl women want to be *and* want to be friends with."

"Um, thank you." Lucy's raised inflection hinted at her confusion. She had no idea where this conversation was going.

"But I had to make sure you were the real deal," Morgan continued with an air of pretentious authority. "People can fake a lot on camera. There are filters, lighting illusions, editing tricks. Not to mention, some so-called influencers will record a video a hundred times for one good take. We don't have time for that. Which is why I needed to see you in action. Call it an audition of sorts."

"An audition?"

Morgan's red lips stretched to showcase her straight, startling white teeth. "My client, Trent Luxe, is producing and starring in a new reality TV show called *Live, Laugh, Luxe*. And he needs a costar. A sexy sidekick, if you will. He wants someone unknown who can hold her own around the elite and wealthy, since the entire show will revolve around Trent and his costar traveling the world, indulging in obscene luxuries. I think you'll handle yourself beautifully. And we already know the camera loves you."

Morgan continued to simper as though she'd just offered her the entire world on a silver platter. And, in a way, Lucy supposed that she had, but she was still too shocked to respond. They seriously wanted her to travel the globe with Trent Luxe? It didn't seem real.

"Before we sign any papers," Morgan added, "Trent would like to meet you himself, to make sure the two of you click. We'll send a private plane to pick you up tomorrow afternoon for a lunch date in LA. I'll be in touch, but if you have any questions before then, give me a call." She slipped a business card out of her beaded clutch and handed it to Lucy. "I don't need to tell you that opportunities like this don't come around every day. Some of the other producers wanted to go with a trained actress, but I stuck my neck out for you. Don't let me down."

She disappeared inside, leaving Lucy alone to regain her footing in the aftershock.

It seemed too good to be true. She'd be paid to travel in luxury to the world's most exotic locations? For someone who had no idea what to do with her life, it wasn't an entirely distasteful option.

Especially if her life would no longer include Vick.

At the thought, a tightness spread across her chest, and her eyes burned.

Faced with unbearable heartache, was the chance to escape exactly what she needed?

CHAPTER 25

Early the next morning, Lucy plodded down the back steps of the inn, her thick-soled boots heavier than normal.

The golden mid-morning sun tried to lift her spirits, but to no avail. Too many troubled thoughts spiraled in her head.

As she crossed the backyard, she ignored the remnants of last night's party yet to be packed away. Each bare table and stray chair reminded her that Vick never showed, triggering her pain anew.

Part of her wanted to immediately dismiss Morgan's offer, seek out Vick, and find out why he never responded to her note. But another, louder voice reasoned that meeting Trent couldn't hurt.

If things with Vick were beyond repair, she'd have a viable alternative, a chance to get away from it all.

Even the mere possibility made her chest hurt, like running too far, too fast and forgetting to breathe.

Her cell phone buzzed, and she paused by the gazebo to retrieve it from her coat pocket.

She read the text from Morgan twice, trying to wrap her head around the surreal message. She'd need to be at the private airport in Primrose Valley in less than an hour, then she'd be on her way to meet the man she may or may not be joining on a tour around the globe for several months.

In a different lifetime, she might find the opportunity thrilling. And if she concentrated hard enough, the siren call of extravagant adventures might come close to igniting her imagination and wanderlust. But she couldn't bring herself to be excited, not when she thought about everything she'd be leaving behind.

Especially Vick.

The uncomfortable tension spread across her chest again, and she struggled to inhale a deep breath.

Even in the expansive outdoors, with fresh, crisp air in endless supply, invisible walls closed in around her, reminding her that so much of her life remained uncertain.

What if they discovered something on the MRI and whatever choices she once had were suddenly stripped away?

Part of the arrangement for meeting Trent gave her access to his private pilot and driver for the afternoon, so she'd scheduled the return flight for after her doctor's appointment.

The downside was that no one else could come with her, which generated plenty of grumbling from Jack and Sadie in particular. Lucy loved them for it and didn't want to hurt their feelings by confessing the one person she wanted by her side the most had already let her down.

Slipping her phone back into her coat pocket, she ducked down the narrow trail leading into the forest of fragrant pines and sinewy sycamores, forcing the bleak reflections aside.

The farther she headed into the woods, following Kat's directions from memory, the softer her footfalls became, as if the dense, protective covering offered shelter from her troubles.

When she rounded the bend in the well-traversed path, she

came to a small clearing with a single bench in the heart of the thicket.

Jayla sat in the middle, her head tilted back, gazing up at the swaying branches.

Surprised to not be alone, Lucy stepped back, snapping a twig beneath her heel.

Jayla jumped, then smiled when she caught sight of Lucy. "Hi."

"I'm sorry to interrupt. I'll—"

"Join me. There's plenty of room." Jayla scooted to the side, leaving the center of the bench open for Lucy.

"Are you sure? I really don't mind coming back later."

"I insist." Jayla patted the smooth cedar slats, and Lucy settled beside her, grateful for the invitation. She wasn't sure why, but she had her heart set on visiting this spot today.

"So, what's so special about—" Lucy's question stalled on the tip of her tongue, her gaze drawn upward by an unexpected, ethereal sound.

Lyrical wind danced through the tops of the trees, seemingly coming from every direction. Frozen in wonder, she held her breath, as though a single utterance would disturb the magical corner of the universe suspended in time and space.

"Beautiful, isn't it?" Jayla asked softly.

"I've never heard anything like it," Lucy whispered. "How is it possible?"

"I don't know. A small convergence zone, maybe? Or more likely a trick of the ear. I thought about looking it up, but didn't want to spoil the illusion."

"I can see why Kat loves it here."

"Me, too. I've been back several times since my first visit."

Lucy noticed something had shifted in Jayla's demeanor, or maybe her countenance, and without thinking, she asked, "Has it helped?"

"It sounds strange, but yes. I think it has. Or maybe the wind just confirmed what I already knew." She released a light, incredulous laugh, as though she couldn't believe her own logic. "For weeks, I'd been questioning how much longer I could do my job, if I needed to quit. I was tired and burnt out. But sitting here, I realized I could never give it up. It brings me joy and a sense of purpose. I just need to be better about taking breaks and asking for help."

"A sense of purpose," Lucy murmured, studying the slivers of sky peeking through the branches. "I wish I knew how to find mine."

For several seconds, Jayla didn't respond. When she finally spoke, her words were gentle and carefully considered. "Perhaps it's been there all along, but there's something keeping you from seeing it?"

"Maybe," Lucy conceded, though it didn't seem likely. "How did you find yours?"

"Honestly, it came about kind of like this place. The convergence of life's opportunities, what I was good at, what brought me joy, and what allowed me to bless others. All the pieces pointed to the same thing."

"And what you do is incredible, Jayla," Lucy told her with genuine admiration.

To her surprise, Jayla shrugged off the compliment. "It's no more noble than what anyone else does. We all have the ability and opportunity to make a difference in our own unique way. Like you, Lucy. You have a special gift. A voice. There's something about you that draws people in and inspires them to act. Real, genuine influence from a place of kindness and humility. And I have no doubt you'll figure out exactly what to do with it." She gave her shoulder a squeeze before rising from the bench. "Sometimes, all you have to do is wait for a subtle whisper in the wind."

With one last smile, she waved goodbye and disappeared down the path toward the inn, leaving Lucy alone on the bench.

Inhaling a deep, cleansing breath, she closed her eyes and opened her heart, finally prepared to listen.

~

Vick sat in his Jeep, the engine idling.

Parked outside his home, he hadn't budged for over five minutes, torn between confronting Rhett and going after Lucy.

In the wake of his encounter with Rhett last night, he'd been too rattled to stay. He'd needed answers. After making several calls, he'd finally gotten a hold of their old neighbor in Los Angeles, Lisa Alinac, who confirmed Rhett's story. At least, the part about Rhett being his father.

He still couldn't believe it.

What he knew about the hardworking, amiable cook didn't fit the picture of his deadbeat dad. And he resented being filled with so many questions about his past—questions he'd purposefully buried.

At a young age, he'd resolved to never look for his father.

Now that the man was right in front of him, he didn't know what to do.

He thought about what Rhett said regarding his parole officer. She obviously knew he was in town somewhere; she simply needed to catch him by surprise. How would he feel if Rhett got hauled away without ever seeing him again? Did he even want to talk?

He still wasn't sure.

But he *was* sure how he felt about Lucy. And he wanted to hear her side of the story, to know why that other man had been at the party with her.

Maybe it wasn't as bad as it looked?

He prayed that it wasn't.

Pulling out of his parking spot, he eased down the dirt road, being mindful of meandering chickens. He'd already talked to Bill about switching from a month-to-month agreement to a year-long lease, and he'd been touched by how readily Bill agreed. He even mentioned how broken-up Buddy would be if he left. Although his four-legged friend had been spending a lot of time with another goat named Holly, proving even Buddy knew more about love than he did. Maybe he should ask for a few pointers? Especially if his rival Peter Pan stood half a chance.

Beyond the gate, Vick stepped on the gas, suddenly in more of a hurry.

When he pulled into the driveway of the inn, Sadie was unloading boxes of chocolate from the back of her delivery van.

Vick hopped out of the Jeep to help her. "Have you seen Lucy today?" Her car wasn't parked in the driveway.

"Earlier this morning. But she's on her way to LA right now."

"What?" His heartbeat stalled, and he leaned against the side of the van to gather a breath. At the news, everything inside of him ached with regret and defeat.

The neurological clinic was in LA, which meant she'd finally made her appointment. More than anything, he'd wanted to go with her, to be a steady presence, a shoulder to lean on, the support she needed.

But he'd missed his chance.

As if sensing the weight of his disappointment, Sadie set down her stack of boxes and turned to face him, her features soft, yet serious. "Do you love her?"

"Yes, ma'am." He had zero doubt and didn't care who knew it, even in light of his epic failure.

"Then for goodness' sake, please tell her already." The sparkle in her eyes belied the censure in her voice.

"Believe me, I plan on it." Running a hand through his hair, he racked his brain for a solution, something to fix his terrible timing. "Do you know where her appointment is? If I leave right now maybe—"

"You'll never make it if you drive."

"I don't really have another option." Crushing regret wrapped around his chest again.

If only he'd arrived sooner.

Slipping her phone from her back pocket, Sadie smiled. "Lucky for you, I do."

CHAPTER 26

With a surreptitious head tilt, Lucy studied the man sitting across from her. Trent Luxe wasn't anything like what she'd expected. For an entitled heir of a Fortune 500 family who appeared on a sensationalized, drama-filled dating show like *Blind Date a Billionaire,* he exuded a remarkably down-to-earth quality. Which surprised her, considering the entire theme of *Live, Laugh, Luxe* revolved around obscene luxury.

Maybe he wouldn't be as insufferable as she thought?

Sure, he had the kind of flawless skin and teeth only good money could buy, but he wasn't flashy with his wealth, opting for more common clothing brands. Even Morgan's wardrobe had a higher price tag, and she'd nearly blinded Lucy several times throughout lunch with her diamond-studded Cartier watch.

The restaurant itself was also more low-key than Lucy anticipated—a simple vegan café with flute music and a distinct earthy smell. As Trent picked at a salad featuring both wheatgrass and bean sprouts, her mind wandered to Jack's comment from a few days prior, which stirred her simmering anxiety about her impending MRI later that afternoon.

She pushed the unwelcome thought aside, trying to focus on what Trent was saying.

"You remember the trendy catchphrase from a while back? YOLO?"

"Sure. It stands for you only live once."

"Exactly." Trent stabbed his fork in the air for emphasis. "That's the kinda vibe I want for the show. We can have whatever we want, whenever we want, no financial restraints or limitations. You want to sail a superyacht around the Cape of Good Hope? You got it. You want to ski the Swiss Alps and spend the night in an ice castle that looks like the Taj Mahal? You got it. It's about making dreams come true. Whatever you want, we make it happen."

Whatever she wanted....

While his offer sounded tempting, how could she explain that what she wanted most in life couldn't be bought?

"Sounds great." She summoned a smile, glancing between Trent and Morgan. They both looked so excited, but she couldn't match their enthusiasm. In her mind, the extravagant experiences were only part of the equation. The company mattered so much more.

"It sounds *transcendent*," Morgan added, her tone indicating that she didn't think Lucy's adjective did the scenario justice.

"What about my YouTube channel?" Lucy asked. "Can I keep it going?"

"I'm afraid not." Morgan pursed her lips, her frozen features appearing faintly apologetic. "It's a conflict of interest."

"You don't need it." Trent waved away her concern. "You'll be on TV. That's like YouTube on steroids."

Lucy sipped her ginger-infused water to hide her disappointment. Although she never intended for the channel to be a permanent fixture in her life, the idea of letting it go altogether didn't sit well. Could she really give it up?

"There's one other thing." Trent rested his fork on the edge of the plate. "I want to make sure you understand the dynamic I'm going for."

"Of course." Lucy mirrored his movement, the ice clinking as she set down her glass. She'd promised herself to hear him out, although her heart wasn't in the conversation.

While it may be wise, she didn't want a backup plan. She wanted Vick. She wanted to stay in Poppy Creek near her friends and family. She wanted a simple life, with a cozy house, and a cuddly, affectionate dog like Fitz.

Ever since the Pumpkin & Paws event, she couldn't stop thinking about the roly-poly pup who'd captured her heart with her wiggly backside and wrinkled snout. She even thought about naming her Tink, which was more of an ironic name since she certainly wasn't tiny.

But as clearly as the image of her ideal future formed in her mind, it still seemed so out of reach. Maybe even impossible.

At the thought, heat burned behind her eyes, and she blinked, forcing her attention back on Trent.

"I want to make it clear that I'm the voice of the operation," he droned. "The head honcho. Kinda like the host of that old game show my mom likes, *Wheel of Fortune*. The host is the one driving the boat, so to speak. He calls the shots. And no less important," he said with a slightly condescending tone, "is the girl who turns the blank squares around to reveal the letters. What's her name?"

He snapped his fingers at Morgan, who answered with mild annoyance, "Vanna White."

"Right. You'd be Vanna White. Which is the better gig, if you think about it. You get to travel the world, living it up, without getting scorched in the spotlight." He flashed a practiced grin that came all too easily. "So, Lucy-Goosey, whaddya say? Sound good to you?"

Lucy winced at his overfamiliarity.

"Yes, Lucy," Morgan added with a pointed gaze. "What do you think about this once-in-a-lifetime opportunity?"

Suddenly parched, Lucy took another sip of water, ignoring the way the ginger tingled against her throat.

Once in a lifetime indeed.

If it was the life she wanted.

~

Standing to the side of the dirt runway, Vick watched as Colt went over last-minute details with Hunter West. The easygoing cowboy who owned Lupine Ridge Ranch agreed to loan Colt one of his planes for the afternoon.

According to Sadie, he'd done it once before a few summers ago.

A strange warmth spread across Vick's chest when he thought about how many people had come together to make this day happen. Sadie had called Colt, who'd called Hunter about the plane. Jack volunteered to cover for Colt at the restaurant, which meant even more people had to cover for Jack at the diner. All so Vick could make it to LA in time for Lucy's appointment with the specialist.

Although grateful, he wished it could've been achieved by any means other than a small, flimsy aircraft. He'd ride in a beefy military helicopter like the Super Stallion all day, every day. Rotary wings made sense. Light, fixed-wing airplanes? Not so much.

But anything for Lucy.

Before they left for Lupine Ridge, Jack had placed a hand on his shoulder and said, "Take good care of her." His voice had been thick and husky, but Vick recognized the gesture for what it was —his blessing.

In turn, Vick asked Jack to assign Rhett to the back kitchen, rather than the bar up front, without going into the details.

While he still wasn't sure how he wanted to handle things, he wasn't ready for Rhett to disappear—or worse.

"Let's go!" Colt waved him over to the plane, then shook Hunter's hand.

The cowboy tipped his hat and strode a safe distance away to observe the takeoff.

As Vick settled inside the blue-and-white Cessna 172—the plane Hunter used to give aerial tours to ranch guests—Colt rattled off a few safety precautions, appearing perfectly at ease inside the metal death trap. Thankfully, he rented a similar model at the private airport in Primrose Valley once or twice a month to keep up his skills, which offered Vick an ounce of comfort.

Their headsets in place, Colt asked, "Ready?"

Vick gave a thumbs-up, his teeth too clenched to speak. Gathering a deep breath, he focused his mind on Lucy.

The rickety plane rumbled down the runway, gaining speed.

With sweaty palms, Vick gripped the edge of the seat, imagining Lucy's face lit up with excitement, knowing she'd love this. She'd probably make some crack about pixie dust or thinking happy thoughts.

In the span of a single second, the lightweight aircraft popped off the ground, quickly climbing higher into the sky as the ground grew farther away.

Soon, Hunter's hulking frame resembled a tiny dot in the distance, eventually disappearing behind the tops of the trees.

After a few minutes, Vick forgot all about his fear of flying, too engrossed with the jaw-dropping view. Acres of sprawling meadows, glistening lakes, and rugged mountains stretched beneath them like a private panorama.

"Cool, huh?" Colt grinned, dipping the plane's wing for a better angle.

Vick's stomach flipped, but quickly settled. From this height, the fall colors appeared even more striking, vibrant patches of yellows, oranges, and reds intermixed with blues and greens. If all went well, he'd get to share the incredible view with Lucy on the flight back.

Colt planned to hang around LA and visit with an old friend who owned an exotic car dealership, where Colt used to be the top salesman. Not only had his buddy offered to pick them up at the airport, he volunteered to loan Vick a convertible Audi R8 in a metallic gold color to drive around the city, which Vick knew Lucy would enjoy.

With a secretive smile, Vick glanced over his shoulder at the black backpack containing the other part of his plan.

His pulse hummed, eager to see Lucy's expression when she caught sight of him.

He only hoped it wasn't too little too late.

CHAPTER 27

Lucy stood on the cracked sidewalk, staring up at the sleek, modern building.

In comparison, she suddenly felt small and so very, very alone.

You can do this.

Raising her chin, she squared her shoulders, mustering every ounce of courage despite the erratic rhythm of her heartbeat.

What she wouldn't give to hold Vick's hand, to feel the weight of his palm against hers, to inhale the comforting scent of his presence.

She should've called. She should've done something, anything, to make things right.

Maybe it wasn't too late.

Digging through her purse, she found her phone. Although he couldn't be here in person, she longed to hear his voice. Even if only for a fleeting moment.

She unlocked the screen, startled by a thundering car engine. As she turned toward the source of the sound, a shimmering gold convertible slid along the curb, parking a few spots down.

A streak of sunlight glinted off the windshield, obstructing a clear view of the driver. He reached for something in the passenger seat, and seconds later, a jaunty red feather ruffled in the breeze above his head.

Unable to tear her gaze away, she watched him exit the vehicle, her heart pounding. The phone slipped from her hand, clattering inside her purse.

Clad in his Peter Pan costume, complete with fitted tights showcasing his muscular calves, Vick Johnson strode toward her.

Both hands flew to her mouth, barely muffling her gasp.

In mere seconds, he stood before her, his expression tender yet tentative. "I'm sorry I'm late."

"To the party?" she asked with a small, playful smile, still unable to believe her eyes. Could he really be here?

"To everything." His voice filled with meaning, he closed the gap between them.

Her pulse hummed, heat spreading through her as he held her gaze.

"I'm sorry, Luce. I was a coward who probably doesn't deserve a second chance. But if you'll have me, I want to be with you. For all of it, the good and the bad. And I'm never going to leave."

"'Never is an awfully long time.'" In a breathy whisper, she quoted the line from *Peter Pan,* her eyes brimming with happy tears.

"Not long enough." In one swift motion, he gently gathered her face in his hands.

But there was nothing gentle about his kiss, both urgent and vital, like a life-saving breath.

Lucy lost herself in the indescribable sensations washing over every inch of her body, at once shivering yet flushed with warmth.

When Vick finally pulled away, he rested his forehead against hers and murmured, "I love you, Lucy Gardener. I love the way you smile as easily as you breathe. I love that you connect with others, truly seeing the heart of a person. I love the way you notice and appreciate the little things, like the smell of decaying leaves."

She laughed softly. "And I love that you call them decaying leaves."

His breath hitched, and she glanced up, meeting his gaze.

He searched her face, a hopeful glint in his eyes.

Tracing her fingers from his cheekbone down to his stubbled jaw, she confessed, "I love you, too. More than I ever thought possible. And I have a feeling it's only the beginning."

He captured her mouth again, oblivious to the strange stares lobbed in their direction from passersby.

In that moment, nothing else mattered.

She'd found her person.

And no matter what the future held, they'd choose hope... together.

~

Nick stared at Lucy's hand partially hidden beneath his. Her long, delicate fingers gripped his more firmly than before. He couldn't imagine what was going through her mind as they waited in the exam room for the results of the MRI.

Thanks to Dr. Dunlap's personal connection, they only had to wait a few hours rather than days. Or even worse, weeks. How could anyone wait that long for such life-altering news?

Even now, his pulse raced, and his dry throat burned.

He couldn't shake the ominous churn in the pit of his stomach, like something was seriously wrong. His own feelings of fear and loss aside, he'd do anything to shield Lucy from an ounce of the pain his mother must have endured during her illness.

Wasn't that part of what made sickness and disease so cruel? The utter helplessness. The inability to lift the burden from your loved one.

A cold shiver shuddered through him, and he tightened his grip on Lucy's hand.

Whatever the outcome, they'd go through it together.

He'd been given an incredible gift, no matter how much time they had left together. He still couldn't believe she loved him in return, and wanted to be with him despite his shortcomings. For the rest of his life, he'd live in awe of this reality.

She squeezed his hand. "I'm so glad you're here."

"Me, too," he murmured, his voice raw and raspy.

"And you were right, by the way." She smiled up at him. "I never should've tried to go through this on my own. Thank you for being honest with me."

"I just wish I would've been more honest with myself," he admitted. "Or at least, heeded my own advice." He shifted on the stiff chair to face her. "I've been doing life on my own for far too long. And I'm taking big steps to change that."

"You are?"

"Jack is letting me stay at the diner part-time until I settle into my new job."

"New job?" Her eyes widened.

He couldn't help a smile. "As a coffee roaster. Frank wants to retire to spend more time with Beverly."

"He does? Oh, Vick, that's wonderful news!"

Her enthusiasm radiated throughout the sterile hospital room, transforming it into a bright, cozy space. She had a knack for turning the most mundane location into the most spectacular spot in the world.

"I'm so happy for you. You're going to be a fabulous coffee roaster. And Beverly must be thrilled. I don't think any of us believed Frank would ever retire."

"He'll still be around to help out, but the accident was a big wake-up call for him. He realized life is precious and we can't take a single second for granted. If something's important to you, you have to make time for it."

"I've realized that myself recently," she murmured.

He leaned forward, sensing she had more to say.

"I've decided to continue with my YouTube channel," she confessed after releasing a deep, pent-up breath.

"Oh, yeah?" He could feel the grin spread across his face. There wasn't a doubt in his mind that she'd made the right decision.

"I resisted the idea for a long time, not sure how I'd make it work. Or if I even wanted to. But, do you remember Morgan?"

"The guest at the inn?" He wasn't sure where this was going. The woman had always rubbed him the wrong way.

As though reading his mind, she laughed. "I know what you're thinking. She wasn't my favorite person, either. And it turns out, she was in Poppy Creek scouting me for a role on a reality TV show."

"Really?" His heartbeat stuttered, and it must have shown on his face.

"Don't worry." She smiled. "I turned down her offer. I thought she'd be upset, but she took me out for a cup of coffee and gave me great advice on how to monetize my platform and refocus my brand."

"You're kidding." He found a magnanimous Morgan hard to believe, but he did have a history of reading people wrong. Lucy being a prime example.

"I was just as surprised. She said it's important for women in our industry to support each other. So, while she isn't my favorite person in the world, I have a newfound respect for her."

Once again, he admired her ability to see the good in people. "What changes did she suggest you make?"

"An entire overhaul." Her eyes lit up with excitement. "I'm calling it *Grow, with Lucy Gardener.* Educate, motivate, and cultivate your best life with an emphasis on making a difference in the world. My first feature will be on Jayla Moore and the work she's doing across the country. I hope to spread awareness and inspire others with a similar heart and mindset to join the cause."

Her infectious energy brightened her entire countenance, and he couldn't help leaning in for a spontaneous kiss.

When they finally broke apart, she breathlessly asked, "What was that for?"

"Do I need a reason?"

"No, I guess not." She laughed, glowing with happiness.

"But I am proud of you, Luce. You're going to do amazing things."

"I don't know about that." Blushing, she tucked a strand of hair behind her ear. "I just figured I have a platform and a voice I can share with others. So, why not do something with it?"

"If you ever need a camera guy, you know where to find me."

She grinned, and there was that kiss again, tucked in the right-hand corner of her mouth. He couldn't get enough of it.

Cupping her chin, he leaned down, pausing when a throat cleared.

Dr. Patricia Stinwell stood in the doorway, clipboard in hand. "Are you ready for the results?"

Vick searched her stoic features, looking for a clue, a hint, anything.

But found none.

The air in the room shifted, no longer bright and bursting with possibilities.

Tension hung like a heavy cloud, making it difficult to breathe.

In the next moment, everything could change.

CHAPTER 28

Tears of relief filled Lucy's eyes as Dr. Stinwell ruled out her worst fears.

No tumor. No cysts. No hemorrhage, inflammation, or swelling.

Nothing that incited immediate alarm, which was reason enough to rejoice.

Although, they still didn't know what was causing the migraines, so she'd need additional testing. In the meantime, the doctor prescribed her medication to lessen the effects of future episodes.

As they exited the building, arm in arm, Vick asked, "You okay?"

"I am." She smiled, still so grateful to have him by her side during the process. "While I wish we had more answers, I'm relieved it's not one of the scarier possibilities. With those looming fears behind me now, it feels more manageable, somehow."

"I'm glad to hear it. And I have no doubt they'll figure out what's going on soon and come up with a plan to treat it." He gave her hand a reassuring squeeze.

"I'm sure you're right." In the back of her mind, she realized she could have come to this conclusion much sooner if she'd made the appointment when Dr. Dunlap first suggested it. But there wasn't much point in dwelling on the past. Especially when her future looked so bright. But she had a feeling after what she'd learned through this experience, she'd do things differently if she ever faced a similar situation.

She stole a glance at Vick and couldn't help another contented smile. He looked so endearing in the Peter Pan getup, and he'd gallantly ignored all the snickering stares. Even Dr. Stinwell had been taken aback, stumbling over her words when she first caught sight of him, but Vick didn't seem to mind. He'd put his pride aside, communicating his commitment to her in the unexpected and bold choice.

He opened the passenger door to the flashy convertible, but before she slid inside, he kissed her again, slow and tender, until her toes tingled.

When their lips finally parted, she gazed up at him, dazed and more than a little breathless. "I still can't believe you're here. And that you rented this car." Based on the color and convertible top —two things she loved—she assumed he'd planned it as part of his grand gesture. Still, it was a miracle he'd made it in time for her appointment. He must have driven well over the speed limit. Even then, it seemed impossible.

"Technically, I didn't rent it," he admitted. "It's a loan." He waited for her to get settled, then strode around to the driver's side before elaborating on his comment.

She listened in awe as he explained how everyone came together to make sure all the necessary details aligned. And when he shared that Sadie had initiated the chain of events, her heart brimmed with affection and gratitude. What had she ever done to deserve such a wonderful, selfless friend?

"You're going to love the flight home," Vick told her, sounding genuinely excited to share the experience with her.

At his remark, Lucy remembered she needed to cancel Trent's driver and pilot, and dug inside her purse for her phone. She made a quick call, then slipped her phone back in the bag, eager to enjoy the rest of the day.

So much had changed in such a short amount of time, and she still struggled to wrap her head around it. But while her brain found it all astonishing and surreal, her heart had never been more blissfully content. Even the unknown territory of her migraines, and the potentially long road ahead to reach a diagnosis, didn't dissuade her happiness.

With Vick by her side, nothing seemed too big or insurmountable. And each new moment together filled her with fresh hope and excitement.

~

Just as Vick expected, Lucy was enthralled with every aspect of the flight home, from the exhilarating takeoff to the incredible vantage point.

While she said she'd appreciated certain aspects of the private jet, the view couldn't compare to the high-wing Cessna that displayed the entire world below them in a striking tableau of shapes and colors.

Plus, Colt let them both ride in the back seats, which meant they hadn't stopped holding hands since takeoff. Vick didn't think he'd ever get tired of her soft skin against his or the perfect fit of their entwined fingers, which he found both comforting and scintillating.

He'd never had this kind of connection with someone before, and it pushed him out of his comfort zone in the best possible way. In situations he'd normally shut everyone out, he became eager to let down his walls.

"Can I ask for your advice?" He spoke into the headset speaker, directing his question to both Lucy and Colt.

He nearly laughed out loud at the surprised looks on their faces. Apparently, he wasn't the only one still adjusting to his new mindset.

Lucy responded first. "Of course."

He filled them in on what happened the night of the Library Benefit Banquet, reliving some of the shock in their equally stunned reactions.

"Yeesh, man." Colt shook his head in disbelief. "That's quite the sucker punch."

"Tell me about it," Vick muttered.

"Are you okay?" Lucy asked softly, her voice filled with care and concern. He saw in her eyes that now, more than ever, she understood why he hadn't shown up to meet her.

Once again, he marveled at her kind, forgiving heart, grateful to be on the receiving end.

"I'm slowly coming to grips with it," he confessed. "But I don't know what to do. Years ago, I resigned myself to never knowing my father. I was convinced that's the way I wanted it. Now that he's here, asking to be a part of my life, does that change things? Should it? Or do I stick to my original decision?"

"What do you *want* to do?" she asked, as if his gut reaction would lead him in the right direction.

"That's the thing," he admitted with a disappointed sigh. "I can't decide. On one hand, I'm curious. A part of me wants to get to know him. On the other hand, life is simpler without knowing. And what if I try and it doesn't go well?"

She nodded, her features conflicted. "I don't have the right answer," she said after a moment's thought. "But I remember what life was like when Jack wouldn't speak to our dad. They were both miserable. I know the situations aren't the same, but I can't help wondering if you'll regret not giving him a chance."

He let her words sink in. Admittedly, he'd wondered the same thing.

"Lucy's right," Colt interjected, his tone laced with empathy.

"Your dad owned up to his past and wants to make amends. It doesn't sound like he's expecting a free pass, which counts for a lot."

Colt made a valid point, which he needed to consider carefully.

"And for what it's worth," Colt added. "I'd give anything for one more day with my dad."

Something in his inflection—perhaps the lingering pain of loss—spoke to Vick with a new depth. Rhett leaving town, or even going back to prison, was one thing. But what if something worse happened? What if he lost his one and only chance?

Would he be able to live with that?

Now more than ever, he wasn't sure he could.

~

The rest of the flight, Lucy and Colt switched the conversation to lighter topics, giving Vick time to process his thoughts. While, in one sense, she was happy Vick had the opportunity to get to know his father, she knew it must be incredibly difficult for him. But she was proud of him for seeking advice. Colt in particular had a perspective close to the issue, and she could tell Vick had taken his words to heart.

Not for the first time, she marveled at how open Vick had become, especially in comparison to when they first met. It wasn't an overnight change, but he was really making an effort to let people into his life, and she loved him all the more for it.

It also wasn't lost on her that he'd chosen to be here, with her, instead of working through issues with his dad, a life-changing opportunity. He had every excuse to think of himself, but he'd put her first, choosing to be there for her when she needed him. She'd never forget that. And she couldn't wait to get him alone to tell him just how much it meant to her.

Since she'd left her car at the Primrose Valley airport that morning, Colt dropped them off so they could drive home together.

But before they got in the car, Vick asked, "Mind if we make a quick stop before we head back to Poppy Creek?"

"Sure. Where to?"

"It's a surprise." He flashed a grin, both eager and somewhat tentative. "But that means I'll have to drive."

"Okay…" she said slowly, handing him her keys. "So mysterious."

He continued to grin, not giving her so much as a single clue.

Her heart did a funny little pitter-patter as she rounded the car to the passenger side.

What exactly did he have in mind?

CHAPTER 29

When they pulled into the parking lot of Purrs & Paws Animal Shelter, Lucy's heart surged with hope, although her secret wish hardly seemed plausible.

How would Vick even know about it?

He came around to her side and opened the car door, a slow, shy smile stealing over his face.

Was he nervous?

She thought about asking the reason for their visit, but in her breathless anticipation, she couldn't find the words. Her gaze drifted to the front door.

A middle-aged woman with a kind, heart-shaped face and clad in a khaki uniform held a wriggly ball of yellow fur in her arms. "Easy girl, hang on," she clucked, trying to contain the pup's enthusiasm.

Lucy's hand flew to her throat, her heartbeat fluttering wildly. Tears in her eyes, she turned to Vick.

"I know I took a big leap," he admitted, his nerves evident in the creases around his eyes. "And I may have overstepped. But I called the shelter to see if she was still available for adoption.

When I saw you at the Pumpkin & Paws event, I had this feeling you two belonged together. But if you don't—"

Before he got out another word, she threw her arms around his neck. "Thank you, thank you." All of her gratitude poured into her embrace before she pulled back to study his face.

Relief washed over his features, and he broke into a grin. "I think she's eager to see you."

Smiling through her tears, Lucy swiped at her damp cheeks as she turned back around.

The volunteer, who Vick must have informed about their arrival, set the pudgy pup on the front porch.

Immediately, she plodded down the broad steps on her chubby legs, and Lucy laughed as she headed straight for her with a pronounced leftward lean in her adorable strut.

Kneeling on the ground, Lucy scooped her into her arms and nuzzled her soft fur. "Hey, Tink. Do you want to come home with me?"

The dog gave Lucy a slobbery kiss.

"I think that's a yes," Vick chuckled.

"I think so, too." Lucy beamed, beyond blissful. As she stood beside Vick, holding the bundle of cuteness in her arms, her heart had never been so full. And to think, Vick had made it all happen.

She caught his eye and mouthed, Thank you, suddenly too overcome with emotion to speak.

A meaningful look passed between them, and like all those times she studied the photographs Vick had taken of her, she felt wholly and deeply seen. As if he knew what she needed even more than she did.

Regretfully, she tore her gaze from his and focused on the shelter volunteer. "Is there paperwork I need to fill out?"

"It's already been taken care of." The woman smiled at Vick. "I'll give you these, and you're all set." She handed Lucy a pink leash and a fuzzy green crocodile with a squeaker inside. "It's her favorite toy."

"Thank you." Lucy tucked the doll beside Tink in her arms, and the little pup prodded it with her soft, wrinkly head.

"Congratulations," the woman told her. "You make a very lovely family." With one last scratch behind Tink's ear, she headed back inside.

Lucy glanced from the pup to Vick, still dressed in his Peter Pan costume, and she had to agree.

Not the most conventional family on the planet, but in her humble opinion, most definitely the best one.

~

Saying goodbye to Lucy had never been so difficult, but at least he had the assurance that she'd be spending the rest of the evening getting Tink settled. Plus, Jack, Kat, and Sadie were on their way over, and Lucy had promised to call her mother with an update as soon as she got home.

Vick squelched a tiny twinge of irritation at the mention of Lucy's mother, since Lucy had explained her intentions with the mysterious Peter Pan. But Lucy assured him that her mother would happily put aside her matchmaking efforts and accept Vick with open arms, and he chose to match her optimism. In fact, he looked forward to meeting her family.

And as much as he wanted to stay by her side tonight, he had somewhere he needed to be.

The entire drive out to Old Highway, he rehearsed what he wanted to say when he arrived. He only hoped he could find the right location.

Nightfall had blanketed the dirt road in darkness, and he relied on his headlights to warn him of impending potholes and fallen branches.

No one ever drove Old Highway anymore, not since the new highway had been built above it, with a bridge to circumvent the regular flooding of the creek below. And even with heavy duty, thick-tread tires, he wasn't sure how much longer his shocks could endure the abuse.

Finally, at the bottom of the hill by the water's edge, he spotted a soft glow in the distance. A shabby camping trailer sat by a dilapidated pickup truck, but the owner had done what he could to spruce up the place. A single strand of string lights stretched from the tattered awning to a nearby tree. Two dingy folding chairs sat around a fire ring made of river rock and sand, a warm fire crackling in the center.

Vick parked and hopped out of the Jeep.

The sound of the trickling stream blended with the crackle of a Harry Chapin song emanating from ancient speakers inside the trailer.

Rhett emerged with an amber bottle in hand, freezing on the bottom step when he spotted Vick.

"Nice place," Vick offered by way of greeting, surprised he actually meant it. Some might only see the flaws, but he saw a man who took pride in what he owned.

"Thanks. It's not much, but it's home. Working on fixing it up a bit."

They stood in awkward silence for what felt like centuries, although it probably only lasted several seconds. And without a natural segue, he blurted the first thing that sprang to mind. "Did you love her?"

Rhett blinked. "Your mother?"

Vick dipped his head in response.

Rhett didn't hesitate before answering, "More than anything. I loved you, too. Even though our most formal introduction was feeling you kick inside your mother's stomach."

He offered a small, wistful smile, but Vick didn't reciprocate. He couldn't. This man had never been a part of his life. For as long as he could remember, he'd been the dead beat who left his pregnant mother to fend for herself. And although the circumstances weren't quite what he'd assumed, forgiveness was a difficult trail to forge.

He'd been wrestling with one all-consuming question since Rhett's confession last night. And it wouldn't be an easy one to ask.

Squaring his shoulders, he forced the words through gritted teeth. "If Mom didn't want you in my life, why should I?"

Rhett flinched, as though Vick had physically wounded him, but to his credit, he kept his composure. "Your mom and I hadn't known each other long before we got married. We were young and impulsive, and got pregnant a few months later. Being the foolish kid I was, I let my fear over not being able to provide for my family tempt me into doing something despicable. I think your mom was afraid she'd made a mistake, that she didn't know me at all. And I can't say I blame her. I still can't believe the unforgivable choices I made."

Unforgivable…

The adjective hovered in the air between them. Was it an accurate description?

A part of him wanted to hold onto the bitterness and resentment he'd accumulated since childhood, collecting grievances instead of baseball cards. But he also knew they would weigh him down, eroding the other areas of his life like a corrosive acid.

And as much as he fought against it, a not too small part of his heart wanted to know this man better, wanted to learn more about his history and roots.

Rhett's features strained as he visibly struggled with what to say next. "I can't excuse what I've done, but I've had a long time to grow and learn from my past. I got an online degree, took every job available to me, including working in the prison kitchen, which is where I learned to cook, and I joined a Bible study led by a visiting chaplain that changed my life. I'm not the same man I was. I don't expect you to accept all of this right away, but if you'll let me, I'd like to spend whatever time I have left here getting to know you better."

Vick let his words seep into the crevices surrounding his hurt and anger, weakening the barricade he'd kept around his heart for years. The road to forgiveness wouldn't be easy, but he had a feeling it was one worth taking. "I guess that'd be okay."

Rhett's mouth twitched, as though he was trying to moderate his reaction when he really wanted to whoop with joy. "Why don't you have a seat by the fire, and I'll grab another one." He raised the bottle. "I don't drink, but I've become rather fond of sarsaparilla. Does that work for you?"

"Sure."

Vick watched Rhett disappear inside the trailer, then glanced at the two chairs facing the flickering flames.

He never thought this moment would come. But then, so many things had surprised him recently.

After a lifetime of running, he'd not only found a home, he'd found a family.

Both new and one he'd lost.

CHAPTER 30

THANKSGIVING

Vick stood on the bank of Willow Lake, mesmerized by hundreds of paper lanterns shimmering across the mirrored surface like scattered slivers of the moon and stars.

This was the first time he'd taken part in Poppy Creek's Thanksgiving celebration, and he found each moment more remarkable than the last. After a seam-stretching potluck meal in the town square, everyone gathered at the lake for the Festival of Lights.

He'd heard of similar events before, but in true Poppy Creek fashion, the residents put their own spin on the tradition. Instead of sending wishes and dreams floating across the still water scrawled on the outsides of their paper lanterns, they wrote notes of gratitude. The collective glow illuminated the cold, clear night in a jaw-dropping display of thankfulness.

If he ever needed a reminder that goodness existed in the world, this would do the trick. Every single person, no matter what they'd been through that year, had at least one blessing to share. And to see all the lights mingled together would soften even the most pessimistic heart.

In prior months, he would've struggled for something to

write on his lantern. But now, his problem would be deciding which blessing to choose.

For starters, he still couldn't believe how things had worked out with Rhett. Without knowing the outcome, they'd confronted his parole officer together and explained the situation. Turns out, she'd lost her father to a heart attack earlier that year and had a soft spot for their reconciliation story. With her help, they appealed to a judge known for his leniency, especially during the holidays, and got Rhett's parole sentence cut short. Now, he could stay in Poppy Creek for as long as he wanted as a free man.

While they still had a lot to work through, Vick enjoyed getting to know his father. He also talked about his mother more often, both with Rhett and Lucy. The memories became less painful, even pleasant. And he loved telling Lucy all the little ways she reminded him of his mother. They would've been good friends.

Sometimes, when he was all alone, he'd brag to his mom about Lucy, sharing all the things he admired about her, like her passion to make a difference in the world. He couldn't be more proud of the work she was doing on her YouTube channel, which had taken off even more spectacularly after her rebranding.

It turned out her mission statement resonated with millions of people, inspiring viewers in all walks of life. Even Frank let her interview him for the segment she did on the veteran's shelter in San Francisco. In fact, his video was one of her highest rated, which didn't surprise Vick in the slightest.

Working as Frank's protégé over the last few weeks had been a highlight for Vick, and he'd quickly come to appreciate the older man's eccentricities. Of course, it would take Frank a while to fully relinquish the reins, but Vick relished the learning process. More than that, he'd found a passion he could grow into and make his own.

He finally felt *settled*. He'd even started joining some of the other guys in regular poker nights and fishing trips. Since he left the Marines, he never thought he'd be a part of a friend group again, a community who had his back no matter what. He regretted taking so long to realize how much he needed one.

"Are you going to stand there holding your lantern all night?" Lucy teased, playfully nudging his arm.

He smiled, warmth spreading across his chest at the mere sound of her voice. "I'm taking my time."

"Don't take too long or all the other tea lights will burn out." She gazed up at him, her blue eyes sparkling in the moonlight.

He found himself staring, once again captivated by her beauty. With her features highlighted in the ethereal glimmer of the lanterns, she literally stole his breath. Her golden hair tumbled around her shoulders, fluttering in the crisp breeze. And the edges of her lips tipped upward, teasing him with their hidden kiss.

While he didn't consider himself a sappy guy, he felt a telltale tightness in the back of his throat. Everything about the night was perfect, from the spectacular scenery to the soft music provided by a guitar and violin duet to the hum of happiness radiating through the throng of townspeople gathered together to give thanks.

It suddenly struck him that his long list of blessings could be traced back to a single origin—the day he met Lucy. She was the one who pulled him off his solitary path and made him question his self-destructive decisions.

A gust of wind swept by them again, whispering a simple yet profound truth.

Vick yanked the cap off the pen and scrawled one word on the stiff paper—one word that summed up so much.

Lucy.

Without her, he'd be on the road again, still running from his past.

With her, he finally had hope for the future.

And he couldn't wait to see where it led.

~

Lucy's heart thrummed as Vick scribbled on his lantern. Something in his expression made her skin tingle. "What did you choose?"

He turned his gaze on her, his gray eyes tender yet dark with intensity. "What do you think?" His voice escaped in a raspy rumble that sent a shiver rippling through her.

He leaned forward and cradled the side of her face, his strong fingers splayed against her cheek, grazing her hair. His touch had a special way of making her feel safe and cherished, like he'd never let her go.

Her breath caught as he lowered his mouth to hers, taking his time with his kiss as though everyone else had disappeared.

Would she ever get used to this exhilarating feeling?

Regretfully, he stepped away and strode toward the edge of the bank. Kneeling down, he set the lantern on the emerald water before giving it a gentle shove. It floated toward the others, leaving delicate ripples in its wake.

They stood side by side a moment, silently admiring the breathtaking sight, hands clasped.

"What did you write on yours?" Vick asked, unable to hide his curiosity.

She glanced up at him, her eyes twinkling. "What do you think?"

He grinned, and she sensed another kiss headed her way.

But before Vick had a chance, Jack loudly cleared his throat, drawing their attention along with the rest of the crowd.

With the backdrop of the luminous lake and shrouded mountain range, Jack looked commanding by the water's edge, Fitz seated by his feet and Kat standing by his side. With one arm around her waist, he addressed their friends and family. "In the spirit of Thanksgiving, Kat and I wanted to express our gratitude to each and every one of you. We owe the success of the inn to the support and generosity of our incredible community."

"We couldn't have done it without you," Kat added, beaming with sincerity.

"Special thanks," Jack continued, "to Trudy and George for all their invaluable advice. And to Colt for taking charge of the restaurant."

Lucy turned her gaze on Colt, who stood nearby with Penny. Was it her imagination, or had he straightened a little taller at Jack's recognition?

"Besides the fact that the restaurant gets you out of my hair at the diner," Jack teased, "I couldn't entrust it to a better man. I'm glad to have you onboard."

"I'm honored to be a part of it." The two men nodded at each other in the same way Lucy had witnessed her brothers exchange compliments in the past, clearly trying to keep their cool.

She couldn't help an amused smile at the rare display of mutual admiration.

Jack cleared his throat again, turning in their direction. "We also want to thank Lucy and Vick. I knew the promotional videos were a good idea, but I'd underestimated my own brilliance." He flashed an unabashed grin. "You two went above and beyond, surpassing my expectations. You make a pretty great team."

Vick squeezed her hand, shooting heat up her arm all the way to her cheeks. Even in the cold, she could feel them tinge pink as everyone clapped and hollered in agreement.

"Lastly..." Jack faced Kat, his features softening. "I want to thank the woman whose dream made all of it possible."

A collective gasp echoed through the trees as Jack knelt before her.

Both of Lucy's hands flew to her mouth, but not before a small squeal escaped.

This was it! The moment they'd all been waiting for.

And it couldn't have been more magical.

Their silhouettes were framed in the warm gleam of lantern light, lending an otherworldly quality to the sight. Lucy had never witnessed anything more beautiful, and tears instantly stung the backs of her eyes.

"Katherine Bennet." Jack's deep voice rumbled with emotion. "From the moment you assaulted me on the sidewalk, I knew I wanted to get to know you better. And it didn't take long to realize I wanted to spend the rest of my life learning every minute detail, from the way you butter your pancakes to your biggest hopes and fears."

A solitary tear of happiness slid down Kat's cheek as he cracked open the small wooden box, revealing the exquisite emerald-and-pearl ring Lucy had seen several weeks earlier.

"It also didn't take long," Jack continued, "to realize that you're the kind of woman who can't help but impact the people around her in a positive way. Just through knowing you, you've made me a better man. You encouraged me to reconnect with my family. And more than that, you've become a part of it. If it's okay with you, I'd like to make it official." He lifted the ring from the velvet cushion, holding it up in the moonlight. "Would you make me and Fitz the two luckiest guys on earth by agreeing to be my wife?"

For his part in the proposal, Fitz barked, and Kat laughed through her tears. "Yes! Yes, to both of you."

In the span of a single second, Jack slipped the ring on her finger and scooped her off the ground and into his arms.

Everyone applauded, cheered, and whooped their congratulations, but Lucy couldn't find her voice, too emotional to make a sound as thoughts swirled in her mind, slowly taking shape.

All this time, she'd been looking for meaning in a fulfilling career, but something so clear, so vital, had been in front of her all along.

The people around her were what mattered most—the relationships, connections, and the impact one person could have on another, both big and small. Because love—a deep, unconditional love that extended far beyond romance—could change someone's life. And that, in and of itself, gave her a sense of passion and purpose.

The rest? Abundant blessings upon blessings.

Vick pulled her closer, and she leaned into his warmth, her heart content.

At that moment, the whole earth felt at peace.

Of course, there would always be heartbreak, health struggles, and hardships.

But through it all, there would be Hope.

They could each be a light in the darkness.

And together, they could light up the world.

EPILOGUE

Sadie Hamilton didn't mind being single.

Even now, watching everyone celebrate Kat and Jack's engagement, she felt happy for the couple, but in no way envious or eager to follow their lead.

Being raised by a spirited, globe-trotting grandmother had taught her how to be comfortable in her skin and content on her own. Plus, she had a supportive community and the most generous and loving group of friends. Not to mention a business that took most of her time. Especially as they headed into the Christmas season, followed by the Food & Beverage Festival, then Valentine's Day. For the next few months, she'd have her hands full—and covered in chocolate.

Thank goodness, too. After she depleted her savings to buy new equipment, her Monday bookkeeping sessions had become depressing. She needed an uptick in business, desperately. Losing the Sweet Shop wasn't an option. Her grandmother had built it from nothing when Sadie was born, even naming it after her with the intent to pass on her legacy.

Sadie couldn't let her down.

She smiled as her grandmother sashayed through the crowd

carrying two steaming cups of Sadie's homemade apple cider. Even with her petite frame, Brigitte "Gigi" Durand knew how to command attention. She wore a long cloak in the most luxurious purple velvet with feather trim dusting the ground. Her fiery red hair—that would never pass as natural—fluttered on top of her head in a mass of wild curls pinned in place by bejeweled berrettes. Sure, some people considered her eccentric fashion choices over the top for an eighty-three-year-old grandmother, but Sadie thought she looked fabulous. In fact, she admired her in every single way.

"You outdid yourself tonight, my dear." Gigi passed her one of the paper cups. "Did you add extra cinnamon to the recipe?" She sipped the cider, smacking her bold red lips as she tried to pinpoint the flavor notes.

"I did. Freshly ground and cinnamon sticks." Sadie wasn't surprised her grandmother noticed. The woman had a palate like no one else she knew, honed after several years of living in Paris. She'd trained under the most prestigious chocolatier, who, according to Gigi, fell hopelessly in love with her in a matter of minutes. Of course, she did tend to embellish a smidge.

"Excellent decision." Gigi nodded, taking another sip. "Did you know that at one point in Ancient Egypt, cinnamon was more valuable than gold?"

"No, I didn't." Sadie hid a smile behind the rim of the cup, always amused by her grandmother's random facts.

"Did you know it's also considered an aphrodisiac?" Gigi asked with utmost innocence.

Sadie sputtered, spewing hot cider down the front of her pea coat.

"Actually," Gigi added, oblivious to Sadie's stunned reaction, "that gives me an idea. We could whip up some cinnamon chocolates and market them on Valentine's Day to all the amorous husbands. What do you think?"

"It's something to consider," Sadie said with as much composure as she could muster.

Even though Gigi retired years ago, handing Sadie the reins to the candy store to travel the world, she never stopped being invested in its success. Luckily, she never looked at the accounting records.

"Well, we're going to have to start thinking outside the box," Gigi told her in a serious tone. "What with that new business opening next door, we can't afford to play it safe."

Sadie straightened, alarm bells going off. "What new business?"

"I don't know all the details just yet. But someone bought Barney's shoe repair shop, and they have big plans to renovate."

"Into what?" Sadie tried to moderate her voice, although her heart raced wildly.

"I don't know exactly. It's mostly rumors so far. But I heard it's something food related. Maybe even our direct competition."

Sadie's heart sank all the way to the soles of her leather boots. This couldn't be happening. She counted on being the only sweet shop in Poppy Creek. "And Mayor Burns approved it?"

"It appears so. Apparently, the new owner is some big time muckety-muck from the city. You know how Burns loves to rub elbows with important people."

"Unfortunately, I do," she said with a heavy sigh. "And who is the new owner?"

"Not a name I recognized. Mortin. Mortis…"

Her blood chilled.

No.... It couldn't be....

"It's not Morris, is it?" she asked with more than a hint of trepidation.

"Yes, that's it!" Gigi snapped her gloved fingers, more for effect than the nonexistent sound. "Landon Morris. How did you know?"

Sadie gritted her teeth. "He's been in town a few times." She internally cringed, thinking of their last encounter.

She'd accidentally stumbled across Landon and another guest, Morgan Withers, outside the inn a few weeks ago. Landon was gently letting Morgan down after the woman's several overt attempts to secure a date with one of the country's most eligible bachelors. To his credit, Landon was kind yet firm. Fortunately, Morgan seemed to take the rejection in stride.

Sadie hoped to sneak away unnoticed, but before she had a chance, Landon glanced in her direction, catching her eye. A tense current sizzled between them, and, to her horror, she'd turned bright red. She couldn't escape to her van fast enough. The whole situation was so embarrassing.

And now, it seemed, the mortification would continue.

Why on earth would he open a business in Poppy Creek? And in direct competition with her candy shop? It didn't make sense. The man hated sugar and sweets of any kind.

If she was lucky, everything he sold would be sugar free.

"Don't look so nervous, *mon amour*. No one makes chocolates like you."

Gigi pinched her cheek, and Sadie had to smile. "I learned from the best."

"And so did I. Which is why you have nothing to worry about."

"Of course, I know you're right. I guess I'm just surprised. Why would someone like Landon Morris want to open a business here?"

"Who knows?" Gigi shrugged. "But I suppose Poppy Creek does have a certain *je ne sais quoi.*"

"That's true, but it still seems strange." Sadie frowned. While Landon wouldn't be the first affluent businessman to settle in a rural area for a change of pace, she still wasn't buying it. Something else had to be going on.

"Well, something about the town must have piqued his interest," Gigi said simply. "Rumor is, he bought that enormous mansion on the other side of the lake."

"What?" Sadie nearly dropped her cup of cider. "From the Zimmermans?"

"That's what I heard."

"I don't believe it." The rambling stone estate had been in Maureen Zimmerman's family for years. Even though the couple now spent most of their time in Florida, she didn't think they'd ever sell the place. Rent it, maybe. But give it up all together? Never.

None of it made any sense.

And none of it was good news.

Not for her business.

Or for her heart.

WANT TO KNOW WHAT HAPPENS NEXT? Join the Secret Garden Cub at rachaelbloome.com and gain early access to the release date of The Hope in Hot Chocolate and download hours of FREE exclusive bonus content.

ACKNOWLEDGMENTS

I can't believe this is book six! In some ways, it feels like my writing journey has only just begun. In other ways, I can't remember a day when I wasn't writing this series. And I owe it all to you, dear reader, for allowing me to share these stories and characters with you.

I'd also like to thank my professional team, Ana Grigoriu-Voicu with Books-design, Beth Attwood editing, Krista Dapkey with KD Proofreading, Cindy Jackson, Trenda London, and Laura Perry. It truly takes a village to get a novel ready for publication, and I have the best team.

And special thanks to author friends Dave Cenker and Daria White, plus my incredible sprinting family on Clubhouse who helped me push through the tough times.

Of course, I wouldn't be able to pursue this dream without the unconditional support of my family, particularly Mr. Bloome. It's been quite the rollercoaster of change in our household, and the support and encouragement of my loved ones has been invaluable.

I'm continually reminded of the power of community.

Thank you for being a part of mine.
I can't wait to see what the future holds…

ABOUT THE AUTHOR

Rachael Bloome is a *hopeful* romantic. She loves every moment leading up to the first kiss, as well as each second after saying, "I do." Torn between her small-town roots and her passion for traveling the world, she weaves both into her stories—and her life!

Joyfully living in her very own love story, she enjoys spending time with her husband and two rescue dogs, Finley and Monkey. When she's not writing, helping to run the family coffee roasting business, or getting together with friends, she's busy planning their next big adventure!

SADIE'S SPICED APPLE CIDER

RECIPE BY MADISON POTEMPA, SUBMITTED BY PEGGY POTEMPA

In keeping with the themes of friendship, family, and community, I asked readers to share their favorite original fall recipes along with the special memories associated with them. It wasn't easy sorting through the myriad of delectable desserts, but I narrowed it down to two, and they became the inspiration behind some of the sweet treats mentioned in the novel. I hope you enjoy them as much as I have!

~Rachael Bloome

From reader, Peggy:

A few years ago, my youngest daughter, Madison Potempa, wanted to have her friends from high school over for a "Fall Fest." She came up with the menu and we shopped, but on that day she did all the cooking (I was laid up with a sudden onset of Ménière's disease, so I was unable to help). I smelled the cider all day and finally came out of my room to try it. Wow! I loved it. I have made something similar since, but nothing as good as hers.

RECIPE

Ingredients:

1 gallon organic apple cider, not juice

1 navel orange, washed

5 or 6 whole cloves

1 Tbs cinnamon, or 2 - 3 cinnamon sticks

1 tsp nutmeg

3 Tbs honey

Instructions:

1. Pour as much of the cider as you can into a crockpot, leaving 2 inches of space from the top.
2. Add all ingredients except orange. Zest about 1 quarter of the orange, then roll the orange on the counter a little, then slice the rest into 1/4 to 1/2 inch slices and put into crockpot.
3. Crockpot should be on high for the first 30 minutes, then decrease to low temperature with the lid on until serving. You want to start early as it gets better and better the longer the flavor melds.
4. Serve warm with a ladle.

Enjoy!

Additional Notes:

As the spiced apple cider is consumed, you can add more of the organic cider into the crockpot and continue to simmer. At the end of the day, you can strain the mixture and put it back into the jar to store in the refrigerator. Shake before pouring. It can be enjoyed cold or warm. You can use 1/2 gallon for a smaller amount, but trust me, you will enjoy having leftovers!

MAGGIE'S PUMPKIN SPICE CINNAMON ROLLS

RECIPE BY SHANNA JOHNSON

From reader, Shanna:

This is a fun recipe I learned from an older lady in my neighborhood growing up. We used to make them every month in fall and winter. As I got older, I adapted the recipe to fit my tastes and add different flavors depending on the season.

Ingredients for dough:

3 cups milk

3/4 cup butter

3/4 cup granulated sugar

1 Tbs salt

3 Tbs yeast

3/4 cup water

3 eggs, slightly beaten

12-13 cups flour

Instructions:

1. Scald milk mixed with butter and sugar until butter is just melted. Set

aside to cool to about 110 degrees, then stir in salt.

2. In a separate bowl, combine yeast and warm water to proof yeast until bubbly.

3. In a large mixing bowl, combine cooled milk mixture, yeast mixture, and beaten eggs. Gradually add flour until dough is elastic and smooth. (You will likely have to take the dough out of the bowl before it gets to this stage and knead in remaining flour.)

4. Spray a clean, large bowl with vegetable oil and add dough. Let rise until double, about 1-1.5 hours.

5. Punch down in center. Divide dough into 4 equal pieces. Roll each section into a 1/2" thick rectangle shape.

Ingredients for filling:

1/3 cup butter (approximately)

3 cups sugar (white or brown)

1/2 cup cinnamon

1/4 cup pumpkin pie spice

Instructions:

1. Melt butter and brush a layer onto the dough. Mix sugar, cinnamon, and pumpkin pie spice. Sprinkle over the dough until the butter absorbs all of the mixture and it is almost dry.

2. Once filling is spread, roll up the dough into a log shape. Pinch off the seam on the long side. Use unflavored/no wax dental floss to cut twelve rolls out of the log (wrap floss around the log and pull; it will cut nicely).

3. Place onto greased baking sheet and bake at 375° F for 12-15 minutes (temperature and time may vary based on location and elevation).

Ingredients for glaze:

3 cups powdered sugar (approximately)

4 Tbs melted butter

1 tsp vanilla

2 tsp pumpkin pie spice

Milk to desired consistency

Instructions:

1. Combine all ingredients.

2. Let the rolls cool for about 10 minutes before pouring the glaze evenly over the rolls. Spread well.

Enjoy!

BOOK CLUB QUESTIONS

1. Which of the fall events was your favorite and why?

2. How did you see the community play a role in the lives of Vick and Lucy?

3. What did you think of Lucy's decision to delay her MRI? How would you react if faced with a similar situation?

4. When did you first suspect Rhett might be Vick's father? Or did the revelation catch you by surprise?

5. How did you feel about Vick's reaction to Rhett being his father? Did you agree with his decision to forgive him? Why or why not?

6. How would you describe the overall theme of the novel?

7. Could you relate to any of the characters? In what ways?

8. Food plays a major role in Poppy Creek activities. Which of the treats mentioned in the novel appealed to you the most? Do you have a favorite fall recipe?

9. Did you have a favorite scene? If so, why was it your favorite?

10. In what ways did you see Vick and Lucy grow over the course of the novel?

As always, I look forward to hearing your thoughts on the story. You can email your responses (or ask your own questions) at hello@rachaelbloome.com or post them in my private Facebook group, Rachael Bloome's Secret Garden Club.

Made in the USA
Columbia, SC
28 December 2021

52904921R00138